Manzanita Seed

Edward Goodman

Plain View Press
http://plainviewpress.net

3800 N. Lamar, Suite 730-260
Austin, TX 78756

ISBN: 978-1-935514-89-3
Library of Congress Control Number: 2011945454

Cover art: Edward Goodman
Cover design by Pam Knight

Acknowledgements

While writing this book was a labor of love, it was also incredibly challenging. I want to offer my deep thanks to my partner Ennio, who first read my rough draft, my siblings Philip and Janis, who meticulously proofread my manuscript and offered encouragement, my late father Morris, who kept me writing by weekly inquiring, "How's your book?" and to my late mother Lillian, whose relentless courage has inspired me my entire life. Lastly, to my beloved dogs Homer, Chata, Frasier, Ozzie, Alex Marie and, of course, Lupe, who have given me an abundance of joy, friendship and love.

To Lupe,

and all the dogs who change our lives

Chapter 1

My name is Anastasio Quintana, and tomorrow I plan to leave the small town in New Mexico where I have spent my entire life. Why I am leaving after all this time is quite complicated and somewhat surprising. I would like to share my story with you.

I am now 62 years old. When my hair started to turn gray about five years ago, most people around my town started calling me Don Tacho. "Tacho" is a nickname for Anastasio and "Don" is a routine sign of respect, an honor bestowed upon men who has simply endured into old age. Don Tacho is a name I may never hear again once I leave this place, but to tell the truth, I have heard little mention of it over most of the past year.

I have lived all of my 62 years in northern New Mexico, in the small town of San Sebastian, which lies ten or fifteen miles north of Albuquerque on the way to Santa Fe. San Sebastian is situated along the Rio Grande River and has been in existence for hundreds of years, many decades before even Albuquerque was founded in 1706. But, while Albuquerque has continued to expand and prosper over the centuries, San Sebastian has barely grown at all.

Things change very slowly here and it is only fairly recently that folks have been able to earn a living doing things other than farming. Despite my sometimes desperate desire to leave San Sebastian over these many years, I have continued to stay here, never living more than a few miles from where I was born.

San Sebastian (pronounced Sahn Sebahs-tee-ahn) was named after the ancient Christian martyr who was rumored to be able to shield people from the plague. He must have been watching over us through the centuries because no one in this town, to my knowledge, has ever come down with the plague.

Our town is not a big place and I suspect it actually has more horses, goats and cows than people. Most of the families here have known each other for generations, since the Spaniards first arrived sometime in the 1500's. The majority of us are related in some way, sharing last names like Lucero, Baca, Chavez and Lujan. We have been a great support for each other in tough times, but our closeness has also stirred up a lot of anger, resentment, fear and gossip. It is a place of few surprises.

As a child, I often wondered what life would be like living on the edge of an ocean, or amidst the tall buildings of a bustling eastern city, or even in a foreign country where people spent hours laughing together at outdoor cafes. But these were just daydreams, nothing more, often borne of boredom and frustration at having one day follow another, each pretty much the same as the one before it.

Later on, when I came to realize that there was simply no escape from San Sebastian, these desperate fantasies were fueled by liquor. Blurry nights of drunkenness, brave loud resolutions to become famous or rich, to invent something important or to explore Himalayan mountaintops. The far-flung places I dreamt about were always somewhere exotic and completely different from my predictable life here. But, I never did leave and before I realized it, I grew old.

Mind you, San Sebastian has given me some proud and happy moments. It is a beautiful place, facing the jagged multi-color Sandia Mountain to the east and wedged against the green banks of the Rio Grande on the west. The vast empty desert of the Sandia Indian reservation stretches out to the south and the expanse of the Santa Ana tribal lands are to the north.

The people of San Sebastian are mostly Mexican-American, with a light sprinkling of Native Americans and Anglos. The people here are hardworking, friendly, family-oriented, religious, and for the most part, poor. The pace is slow, gossip is a routine pastime, and entertainment is an evening watching the sunset and playing dominos on the front porch. One gets used to the slow rhythm of this town, maybe even seduced by it. Each day promises nothing much new, but one remains safe from the dangers of the unknown.

For most of my life, I did pretty much the same as preceding generations of my family. I dropped out of school to help support my parents, brother and two sisters. I got married to the first girl I ever kissed and had a child soon afterward. And, of course, I worked. In San Sebastian, one is expected to work hard. Exhausting physical work, day after day, until you die. That was my life … ordinary, routine, safe, predictable—without great anticipation or hope but absent complication or worry. A year ago, I was 61, hardened and hopeless, often drunk, without a thought of what tomorrow would bring. Then everything changed in one day. The day I met Lupe.

Chapter 2

Before Lupe came to me, I had spent five years alone. Raquel, my wife of almost 35 years, died suddenly one April day hanging up wet laundry on the clothesline. Her heart simply stopped and she was gone by the time she fell to the ground. I was glad that she did not suffer.

Raquel was a strong woman, a pious churchgoer and a dutiful mother. We were married when I was 21 and she was only 19. We had met when we were very young, our families linked together by history, friendship and blood. As a child, I had scant interest in the skinny girl who said little at neighborhood barbeques and church picnics, except to tell folks that she hoped to become a nun. By the time we were teenagers, I started noticing Raquel's bright smile, long dark brown hair and slender figure.

I think Raquel liked me too. I was quiet and polite, unlike my noisy brother and cousins, and the two of us found we could talk for hours in back of the church, during the times I could persuade Raquel to sneak out of Mass. We would talk about our families, town gossip, school and holidays. I didn't mention my fantasies about life outside San Sebastian because I was certain Raquel would think I was a shiftless dreamer.

I think romantic love itself was relatively unexplored in those days, the idea of compatibility and shared goals, complementary personalities and challenging political conversations. Agreeable surface qualities like politeness, respect for family, a shared religious background and an ethic of hard work were enough to demand of a marriage partner.

After we were married, Raquel became a traditional Mexican-American wife of that time—devout, hardworking, honest and clean. I, in turn, tried at first to be a good husband. I worked hard, learning plumbing from my uncle Enrique, and making sure all the bills were paid for our small apartment. When we could afford it, we would invite our large families over for Sunday dinner. Though I was not yet even 22, I tried to be a "real" man, the kind of man who never questioned his fate, who shouldered his responsibilities without complaint, who didn't ask for more that God gave him. The kind of man I never really wanted to be.

Several years went by, in this endless numbing rhythm, and I became increasingly and desperately unhappy. When I was only 24, my days consisted of long hours of dirty and exhausting work, covering up for the mistakes of my drunken uncle. Then it was dinner, sometimes evening mass at church, and finally sleep. I was burdened with constant worries about paying our bills as well as the pressures of pleasing our intrusive and overbearing families.

I don't know exactly when it first happened, but one day, instead of going right home after work, I was invited to drink with some guys from the shop. I discovered how nice it was to relax, loosen up, to be free from the demands of Raquel or my uncle. By the time I was 25, I drank often, and more frequently alone. I drank beer. I spent money on tequila and cheap wine instead of saving it for new shoes or repairs on my truck. I stayed out late drinking and was tired and hungover the following day. I was unable to stop. When I drank, I felt unburdened, perhaps even hopeful. I laughed, I cried, I talked of red sport cars, Sophia Loren's lips, science fiction and the world beyond San Sebastian. When I wasn't drinking, I was thinking about drinking. When I was drinking, I was thinking about freedom.

After our first few years together, the relationship between Raquel and me slowly fell apart. Not that there was much holding us together in the first place other than obligation and sex. Raquel hated my drinking, did not understand my unhappiness and prayed every day in church for me to reform. Raquel's family quickly developed a deep resentment toward me and spread gossip about how badly I was raised, talk that quickly enraged my own family.

Raquel yelled at first and, when that did not work, began silently berating me, slamming my dinner on the table, locking the bedroom door, staring at me with folded arms and cold eyes. When I did not stop drinking, and later refused to even go to church, Raquel finally became resigned and indignant, barely speaking to me. At the time, divorce for a Catholic family was out of the question, so we endured in angry silence.

Sadly, I soon came to see Raquel as little more than a fixture in the house. She did her cleaning, shopping and laundry. I worked welding pipes and cleaning out clogged drains. We ate dinner together, watched television on Saturday nights and always tried to be busy or preoccupied so as to avoid direct contact. We talked only to negotiate our way around each other. It was a sad life for both of us. I know Raquel expected more and deserved better. I don't know why I was this way. At the time, I worried that I was just not ready to be a man. But I also wanted there to be more to being a man than the l life I knew.

Raquel and I had only one child, a daughter, when we were only married a year. After Maria was born, I think we both knew that we could not raise any more children with so little passion between us. We, of course, could not use birth control the few times in the following years we did manage to find a reason to be together in bed. But, somehow God understood our struggle and did not give us any more children. This, of course, did not sit well with our families, who naturally expected more offspring, and at least one son. We endured their taunting, their pleading and finally their cruel whispers. Our relief, though, overcame our embarrassment.

Maria, my daughter, was always a good girl, a quiet and sweet baby. I loved her desperately the moment I first saw her. She had large brown eyes, always open in astonishment at what she saw around here. She was smart as could be and learned to talk and walk well before other children her age. But as Maria got older, and started recognizing me as her father, I soon found myself becoming afraid. I knew I was a terrible husband, was ashamed of my drinking and felt confused by my anger and disappointment with life. I became fearful that Maria would find out that I was not worthy of being a father to her. So, day after day, I worked and drank and watched Maria from a growing distance, wanting to sweep her up in my arms, but feigning indifference.

Raquel did not encourage my involvement with Maria. To her, of course, I was a godless drunk who would only disappoint and corrupt our child. But, the longer my emotional separation from Maria continued, the sadder I was and the more fearful of her I became.

So, as the years went by, Raquel raised Maria almost single-handedly. Eventually, Maria's young pleas for me to play with her, to read her stories, to come to see her in school plays, became fewer and fewer. By the time she was ten, Maria looked at me like a stranger whose existence only meant disappointment and absence.

There were moments, sometimes fueled by alcohol, when I gathered my strength and believed I could still reach out to my beautiful daughter. At these moments, I wanted to get on my knees weeping, asking her to forgive me and let me try once again to be her "papi." I would become excited, for days, planning a wonderful birthday celebration for Maria. I remember the times I decided I would take her to the Albuquerque zoo to see the elephants, or to an amusement park where I would win a big stuffed animal for her shooting wooden ducks. I dreamt of the smiles and hugs that she would offer for the chance to be alone with her father. But I could never do it. I would watch her, sometimes with the tickets in my hand, unable to move, speak or smile, my heart pounding, my mouth dry. Maria would walk by me without even noticing. I eventually concluded that she hated me. It was too late. I was a bad husband and a rotten father. I was incapable of giving love and did not deserve to receive it.

So, Maria grew up, went to college, moved away to Seattle, and her mother died. And then I was alone. My days continued as before, except that I now shopped, cooked, washed clothes and cleaned. And I could drink in the house.

I worked every day until I was ready to drop, drank beer after beer, watched television and waited for sleep to steal away my depression. I awoke to the promise of another identical empty day and drunken night. On weekends, I would vigorously do the chores, trying not to stop for a minute for fear of finding myself alone with my thoughts. The loneliness was agonizing, yet I felt relief at no longer having to deal with the daily sting of failing others. I was failing myself, of course, but I barely cared about that anymore.

This was my path, and I would have worn it deeper and deeper until I finally plunged to Hell, an old and embittered man. But, on an ordinary day in mid-October, something happened that would change my life forever.

Chapter 3

I remember the day I first met Lupe quite well. It was a bright Saturday morning, the weekend of Columbus Day. The sky was blue and cloudless, a slight breeze rustling the browning cottonwood leaves. I was walking down the main street in San Sebastian, Avenida Bosque, carrying two bags of groceries for the coming week. It was warm out, the wind pushing wisps of gray hair onto my face. The day was still young and there weren't many people yet on the street.

I walked home from the supermarket, a bag tucked into each arm, the same way as I always do—my mind focused on when I would have my first beer of the day. I was about to turn onto my street, when I noticed a rusted tan car pulling noisily up to the opposite curb, about 100 yards away. The car had darkened windows, so I could not see inside. I don't think the occupants noticed me standing still in the deep shade of a large cottonwood.

There was nothing on the other side of the road but a ditch and weeds, so I was curious about why someone would stop there. Half a minute passed with nothing happening, and I was about to resume walking home. But all of a sudden, the passenger side door facing the ditch was flung open and, just as quickly, slammed shut. I couldn't see the far side of the car and didn't know whether someone had gotten out. I then heard the engine roar and the car peeled away down the road, its tires screeching. I watched the jalopy disappear for a moment and then stared at the place it had been parked. Nothing was there. I shrugged and was about to turn my corner when I saw some of the dry grass rustling by the curb. Something was moving.

The rustling would stop and then start again about a foot further along. This happened several times. Curious, I crossed the street and walked toward the ditch, with a suddenly growing fear that someone may have been dumped on the road. My mind started racing. A drug hit? An abducted woman? An abandoned baby? God forbid!

I began running, a loaf of bread bouncing out of the bag onto the road. I ignored it, focused only on the spot where I had seen the grass moving. I hurriedly put my bags on the curb and peered into the tall grass. Again, rustling a few feet away. I walked cautiously toward the noise and then saw, lying amongst the weeds, a large patch of dirty brownish fur. It moved a bit. I kept easing toward it, not so afraid anymore, and slowly parted the grass with my hands. I remember holding my breath.

In front of me, just a couple of feet away, was a matted and emaciated dog, on its belly, trying to crawl forward with its front paws. It was dragging its left hind leg behind it, the leg obviously broken and bent almost sideways. The dog was filthy and I pulled back, thinking it might be dangerous, or even rabid. But then it turned its head to look at me. The dog's brown eyes were opened wide, terrified, and it put its head down on the ground and started to whimper, staring intently at me.

It was a medium-sized dog, maybe thirty to forty pounds, with short mottled brown and white fur, a narrow snout and ears that stood upright halfway, the tips hanging down. It was no discernable breed ... just a mutt, fully grown and probably getting on in years given the bit of silver fur on its chin.

I knelt down, whispering "Good dog, Good dog," "What's the matter boy?" and "Nice puppy." The dog continued to stare at me with its big sad eyes and I slowly reached out with my hand, keeping it low to the ground. The dog's ears pulled back in fear, and it squinted, as if expecting me to strike it. I kept talking softly and calmly, and soon, it let me slowly put my hand on its back. The dog was shivering despite the warm weather and I petted it very gently. The dog just looked at me, in panic, wide-eyed, unblinking.

I looked again at the dog's back leg. It was covered with dried blood. I touched it gently and the dog whimpered, but did not raise its head or avert its gaze. I hesitated for a moment, my wife's voice suddenly appearing in my head, telling me to leave, go home, wash my hands and pray that

I didn't get a disease. But, those thoughts quickly vanished from my mind and, without further thought, I slid my hands underneath the dog and lifted it to my chest. The dog whimpered in pain, even growled, but moved very little. I kept whispering soft reassurances in its ear; "Good dog," "Good boy," and then started to walk toward my street. I saw my groceries sitting on the curb, but walked right past them. I quickened my step. I had to bring this poor dog home.

When I got to my house, I kicked open the door and put the dog on my old grey corduroy couch. Raquel would have killed me for putting a dirty and bloody animal on the furniture. But, I didn't hesitate. I laid the dog carefully on its side and it looked at me once for about five seconds and then laid its head down on the couch cushion and closed its eyes. A sudden blinding fear overcame me that the dog had died. My heart started racing, I began to sweat and a feeling of overwhelming desperation crept over me. But then I noticed the slowly steady rise and fall of its ribcage and I let out a sigh. The dog was alive.

My hands still shaking, my heart beating like a drum, I found the phonebook and looked for a nearby veterinarian. What if they weren't open on Saturday? What if they wanted to put the dog to sleep? What if the dog belonged to someone else and had been stolen? Despite having just rescued the poor animal, the thoughts of losing it were flooding through my mind, terrifying me. For some reasons I didn't yet understand, I *needed* this pathetic creature.

I found an old sheet in the closet and wrapped the dog carefully, trying not to touch the injured leg. The dog still looked at me with those terrified eyes, but made no move to wriggle free. I then noticed that it was female.

I put the dog gently on the front seat of my pickup and drove as fast as I could to the Rio Puerco Emergency Animal Clinic in nearby Rio Rancho. I parked and then literally ran across the lot with the dog cradled in my arms, as fast as my skinny old legs and arthritic knees would carry me.

They took the dog immediately and told me within a half hour that they would have to set and cast the dog's broken leg, give it antibiotics, some fluids and check for heartworm. I explained to the veterinarian how I had come across the dog, and she looked at me sadly, figuring I was probably just a poor local man, a Good Samaritan, who had no means to pay what would likely be a huge veterinary bill. She informed me that, with all the medical care, pills and tests, the bill would be at least

$1000.00, reassuring me that I was not responsible for the dog and could leave it if I wanted. I didn't need to ask her what would happen to the dog if I didn't pay the bill.

I could hear Raquel's voice in my mind again, scolding me about the shame of spending $1,000 on a dirty diseased dog that wasn't even mine. But I pushed her hectoring voice out of my head and told the doctor I would pay. She looked at me for a moment, doubt in her eyes, probably wondering whether an old Latino with faded clothes, broken fingernails and dirty shoes could be telling the truth about having so much money. I quickly pulled out my wallet, extracted my credit card and slammed it on the counter. My voice was quavering and I felt close to tears.

"There! Check it out if you want. I've got the money. Now please … PLEASE help that dog!"

After maybe three hours—I lost track of time—the dog was brought out with a cast on its leg and the veterinary technician gave me detailed instructions about pills, the dog's need for rest, food and water and whatever. I didn't even hear her … I was transfixed by the dog, groggy and limp, its long tongue lolling out of its mouth. The tech told me they would prefer to keep the dog overnight for observation, but I refused. I knew I had to take her home. I did not want her to wake up only to see the bars of a cage or strangers around her. She needed to be with me, and to know that I didn't hurt her and throw her away.

The ride back home was quiet. The dog slept next to me on the front seat and I felt a sense of calm overtake me, a feeling of relief that went well beyond the knowledge that she would survive. I guess, as I look back, I realize that I had found a sense of purpose. A satisfying belief that I would matter to this poor dog. At least I hoped I would.

As I got closer to my house, I passed the local Catholic Church, with its large figure of Our Lady of Guadalupe near the front door. While I had steadily grown apart from the Church over the years, I have always loved Guadalupe, the "patron saint of the Americas." Wearing her blue and red star-filled dress, she was the one who does not judge, who cannot hurt or condemn you, who stands only for compassion and solace. I think that's the reason even young people paint her on their cars or wear T-shirts emblazoned with her image.

I slowed down and paused for a moment in front of the Church, gazing at the Guadalupe's figure, with her outstretched arms, missing fingers, peeling blue paint and scarred concrete. She was, as always, calm and serene, staring ahead toward the Sandia. My eyes were then drawn to the pathetic, bandaged and matted dog lying next to me. I knew immediately that I must name this dog Guadalupe. I would call her Lupe, for short.

After I got home, I sat with Lupe for the next twelve hours. I held up her head to give her water and she finally ate some leftover hamburger meat I had in the freezer. I wiped away the dried blood on her fur with my own towel, the fluffy white cotton one Raquel had reserved only for guests. I could only laugh at the thought of how she would react if she were alive. But I didn't care if the cloth was cashmere or consecrated by the Pope.

I eventually dozed off on the couch and didn't wake up until the soft morning light began streaming through the windows. By mid-morning, Lupe was able to raise herself up so she was lying on her belly. When I carried her outside to urinate, she whimpered, but didn't move, just stared at me with those huge unblinking eyes. She was obviously in pain, but she seemed to know that I hadn't caused it. I kept petting her and calling her by her new name, trying to help her understand that I was trying to help. Lupe kept staring at me, with a wary look of fear and also sadness. Even so, I had the feeling that she still carried a glimmer of hope.

Later on, when I was sitting on the couch with Lupe, eating a sandwich, I suddenly felt her lick my hand. Just one quick lick over my first two knuckles. I broke into a huge smile and fist-pumped the air. Suddenly, and with certainty, I knew that we would be okay.

Over the next few days, I found I couldn't leave Lupe, not even for a minute. I had allowed myself to spend as little time as I could with my wife and daughter during the past 40-odd years. I had ruined friendships and alienated my extended family in order to find peace, alone. Yet, I couldn't tear myself away from this scraggly, junkyard dog. Something drew me to her. Maybe it was the fact that we needed each other.

Chapter 4

I have never owned a dog before. At least not for very long. Raquel had always forbidden it—too much hair on the furniture, accidents in the house, barking, chewing, saliva. I remember bringing home a small white puppy on Maria's 8th birthday, given to me by a coworker who brought a box of puppies to work. I knew this was something Maria wanted more than anything. She had asked for a puppy every Christmas since she was four.

The puppy was black with a white chest, bright-eyed, floppy ears and a tail like a whip curled at the end. It chewed on my fingers and had beautiful honey-colored eyes. I rode home with the little dog next to me in the truck, thinking of how happy Maria would be, how we would play with it in the backyard together, take it for walks. I could watch it fall asleep next to my daughter at night. I was excited about what this dog could represent to Maria and me. Something we could share together. A new beginning …

When I got home, Raquel saw me from the window carrying the puppy up the front walkway. Just as I reached the house, the door flew open and my wife stood there like a gladiator, blocking the doorway. I explained to her that the puppy was for Maria's birthday, that it was a good dog, very calm, but she just scowled and demanded that I return it. She would not allow it in the house. I remember Maria coming up behind Raquel and staring at the puppy with wide eyes and a huge smile. But as she listened to her mother's demands, the smile vanished and I could see she had tears in her eyes. I looked at her, my heart breaking, realizing that I had disappointed her yet again. That's all I am to her, I thought, one big failure.

I took the dog back to work, apologized to my coworker and left feeling angry and ashamed. I couldn't bear to talk to either Maria or Raquel for a week. No mention was ever made again of the dog. It turned out to be a good week for drinking though. Once again, I was able to dream about the different places I could live and wonderful things I could do that weren't found in San Sebastian.

Actually, Lupe was not my first dog. I had a dog when I was about 7 years old. One of my older sisters won a cute little terrier mix in a Church raffle. Part Jack Russell terrier, part something else. In those days, dogs were handed out like cookies or shampoo samples; no shots, papers or references. My mother was like Raquel, she hated dogs, but she let us keep it only since it would shame our family if we rejected something given to us by the Church. However, she refused to let the dog inside. I named him Pepito.

I do not recall my mother, Olga Quintana, as a warm or pleasant woman. She was raised in a chaotic home and always saw change as kind of curse or calamity. From her way of thinking, dogs were dirty animals, like chickens or pigs, and they never came inside, no matter how cold the temperature or miserable the weather. My brother and I built a nice doghouse out of scraps of wood from the lumberyard and lined it with old carpeting to keep Pepito warm during the cold weather. We also enclosed a part of the yard for Pepito to play in with rusted wire fencing given to us by the owner of the local hardware store.

I loved Pepito and would spend more time outside with him than I would inside, whether it was scorching hot or freezing cold. I would often crawl into the doghouse and take naps with him, but if my mother caught me, I would get slapped hard in the face and immediately sent to take a bath. I didn't care about the punishment. It was just the price I had to pay to be with my dog.

Every once in awhile, I would work up the courage to sneak Pepito into my bedroom through the window and make my brother swear not to squeal on me. He never did since he loved Pepito as well. We would sit in the dark with a small flashlight and play with the dog until we both collapsed on our beds and fell asleep, Pepito beside me.

If it was cold out and I was already in bed, and winter nights in San Sebastian can get very cold, I would sneak outside and crawl into the doghouse with my only blanket. I would sit with Pepito until he fell asleep, wrap the blanket around him and then sneak back into the house and cover myself with my winter coat. I often took Pepito for walks past the feed store and the grocery, so proud of my handsome dog. He was, in my young mind, the smartest dog in the world. I had to show him to everyone, from the old librarian, Mrs. Chavez, to all the shopkeepers on Avenida Bosque. I taught Pepito to give a paw and to sit. Even to roll over, though he only did this if I had a really great treat like a piece of chorizo. I wanted everyone to know Pepito was my dog. Now when I think back, I realize that I really wanted the world to know that something loved me.

I had a wonderful year with Pepito, despite the occasional beating I got for bringing him food from my plate or sneaking out of church to play with him. But, one day, I went too far.

On one very cold windy night, I snuck Pepito inside. As usual, he slept next to me in my bed. In the morning, when my brother was still sleeping, I crept out quickly to go to the bathroom. When I returned to our room, the door was wide open and Pepito was nowhere to be found. I ran frantically from room to room, repeatedly whispering his name, and then finally flew down the hall to the kitchen. There was little Pepito, with a plate of tortillas on the floor and my mother at the stove, glaring at me, wordless, fuming. Terrified by her eyes, I kept mumbling how sorry I was and quickly picked up the tortillas and took the dog outside. I suspected that I was supposed to yell at the dog or hit him on the nose with newspaper, but I couldn't. I just hugged him and watched him run to the fence to bark at the neighbor's dog. I could see my mother watching me from the kitchen window, scowling. I figured my father would beat the hell out of me when he came home, but I could take it.

Later the same day, as I was arriving back home from school, I went through the gate to the backyard, waiting for Pepito to leap onto me, barking his high-pitched yelp. But, as I closed the gate, there was nothing but silence. I didn't see Pepito anywhere. I crawled into the doghouse, but it was empty. I called his name, over and over, and started to panic, hyperventilating until I was dizzy and almost fell over. I started to cry, but still managed to call for Pepito, with only a choking hoarse whisper coming out of my throat. It was as if I was having a horrible dream. You know, when you scream for help but no sound comes from your lips?

A moment later my father came to the door and said, "The dog ran away. So, SHUT UP!" He then walked back into the house to drink his beer.

I pursued my father into the house and kept repeating, "When did he get out? How did he get out? Who let him out? Didn't you see him? Did you call anyone? … "

I knew I was being disrespectful to my father, nagging him, pressing him, which no one dared to do, not even my mother. All of a sudden, he turned around, and with all his might slapped me on the side of my head, my ear stinging and my head pounding.

"Go to your room and don't come out," he growled, threatening me with a raised arm and closed fist.

I stood there staring at him with my teeth clenched and my eyes wide. I immediately wanted to hit him, to go into the kitchen and slug my mother, since this was no doubt her fault … I wanted to scream and to throw things, to vent my outrage and my deep anguish. I wanted to kill my parents … I really did. Didn't they know what they had done to me? Didn't they care how I felt? Didn't they understand what had been taken from me?!

I ran to my room and could not stop weeping. I couldn't live without Pepito, I didn't want to wake up tomorrow and not find him waiting for me at the door. I suddenly felt deeply and desperately lonely, forgotten and lost. I cried with my face buried deep into my pillow, since my father would beat me more if he heard me crying … Jorge's sons, after all, were not allowed to cry and certainly not over a dog.

The days after Pepito "disappeared" were sort of a blur to me. I went to school, couldn't listen to anything that was said there and did not talk to anyone, unless of course I was asking them about Pepito. I went into the stores, stopped people on the street and asked if anyone had seen a small black dog with a white chest, with pointed ears and a crooked tail. No one had. I called the dog shelter on a payphone, but they said I would have to come look for myself. The shelter was in Albuquerque, way too far to walk. I finally begged someone, told them I was 8-years-old and couldn't come by myself. After an eternity, someone came to the phone and said coldly, " … no stray black or white dogs brought in."

After several days, I finally stopped asking people about Pepito. I stopped searching around corners and in back yards. It was too painful. I knew Pepito was gone. I also knew that my parents would never tell me what they had done with him. To them, my not knowing his fate was part of my punishment. I continued to go to school, do my chores, go to church and do what my parents told me. But I realize now that my indifference toward them had crossed over into hate and pure rage. I withdrew from the family … I had lost not only my beloved friend and companion, but hope as well. I felt like I had fallen into a deep dark pit and had to resign myself to living there. Of course, as time went on, I still had a few friends, I laughed at times with my brother when he wasn't picking on me and even tried for a short time to play shortstop on the school baseball team. But I had become quiet, sad and a loner. And deliberately invisible.

Lupe slowly got better as the days and weeks passed. She developed a ravenous appetite, loved to sniff around the backyard, dragging her casted leg behind her. She also gradually became more trusting and affectionate toward me. I imagined that Lupe had led a pretty rough life before I found her, and couldn't quite understand how she was able to move past it, looking ahead and not carrying a grudge. I know it sounds ridiculous, but somehow Lupe was just born optimist. Perhaps all dogs are. She lived for the moment, was enthusiastic about everything from eating to playing tug-o-war, and for once, I too had reason to get up in the morning. I had to leave Lupe while I was at work, but she just lounged on the couch and slept most of each day. She was having the charmed dog's life that she never knew could exist.

I often worried about Lupe at work, tried to come home for lunch whenever I could, and couldn't wait to get home at night. Finally, after a month of worry and concern, I decided to quit my job. When I had became eligible for my plumber's union pension a few years earlier, I kept working, unable to bear the thought of staying alone at home all day, with nothing but beer and my dark thoughts. But as time went on, my movements became slower and I developed more and more pain in my knees and back from all the years of crawling under sinks and lifting bathtubs. Now that I had Lupe, I finally **wanted** to retire, relieved at the thought of being freed from stuffed drainpipes, broken pump lines and overflowing toilets. I wasn't going to have as much money, but I knew it didn't matter.

Lupe and I now spent our days taking slow walks during the cool winter weather, playing fetch in the backyard, watching television together at night. I even started to cut back on my drinking. I had become irrationally afraid that, if I became stone cold drunk (which wasn't that unusual), Lupe would run away, be hurt by a falling bookcase, fall down the back steps, be bitten by a scorpion or simply be gone when I sobered up. It was crazy. It made no sense. But I didn't want to be alone again.

One day, I decided I had to stop drinking altogether. I still craved alcohol of course, but I just didn't want to be in a state of "unawareness" anymore. Because of Lupe, my need for escape and numbness had greatly diminished.

Withdrawal was, as I expected, miserable, hideous and horrible. But Lupe stayed by my side throughout the long days of vomiting, sweating, screaming, and shaking until I finally started to feel better physically. I had done something I didn't think I could ever do, become sober again.

Soon, I started to invite old friends over the house, to reconnect with a few of my cousins, and even found myself singing in the shower! I had never done that before. I started buying new clothes, at Goodwill mind you, but they were clean and colorful. I bought vanilla milkshakes at Sonic and a Godiva chocolate bar at the new convenience store down the block. I took down all of my wife's stern religious saints, peering judgmentally down at me, and put up posters by Diego Rivera and Frida Kahlo, of men and women dancing and laughing.

I had finally found love in my life. I don't know that I ever had before and it was new and exciting. I stopped dreaming about living in the Swiss Alps or on an island in the South Pacific, and found I was actually looking forward to waking up each morning. In San Sebastian. In my house. With Lupe.

Chapter 5

When I was about 15, I discovered that I loved to read. I think this was borne out of my loneliness and desire for escape. Prior to that, there was rarely any time to read in our house, with the chores, church and school. My father would have considered it to be unmanly to spend time reading novels when you could be cleaning the yard or taking out the priest's garbage. My mother would have simply called it a waste of time. So I just read when I had to, for school assignments.

During my second year of high school, I got a part time job working as a stock boy at Vigil's Mercantile, my father taking most of the money I earned. But I didn't care, because in the back room of the store, I had noticed that there was a huge pile of books in the corner. Beautiful books with leather covers and gold leaf titles. Mr. Vigil told me that a friend of his had stored them there, but had died, and I could throw them away if I wanted. But I kept them all, neatly shelved on two boards I put up in the corner.

One by one, after I finished my work, I would go back to the storeroom and read these wonderful stories—*Call of the Wild, To Kill a Mockingbird, The Old Man and the Sea*, even *Lolita* by Vladimir Nabkov. I was always a fairly good student and fast reader, but had never realized how much enjoyment one could have alone with a book, absorbing the colorful words of a hero from long ago, or discovering the customs and habits of distant and exotic places.

I was fascinated with the saga of John Thornton in the frozen wilderness of Alaska, the tale of Scout and Jem in the segregated South and even the story of Victorian Meg and her sisters in Little Women. Once I went through all the books in the storeroom, I discovered the small San Sebastian library in back of the county farm office and I became a constant visitor there. I never shared my love of reading with the other people in my life … my wife, my daughter, my parents or my friends. It was a secret joy, another exit from San Sebastian and the mundane and painful reality of life. Once I started drinking, of course, my reading slacked off. And I started to prefer drinking to just about anything. But I still managed to sneak in a good book during the times I wasn't at work, asleep or drunk.

My voracious reading had eventually lent itself to an improved vocabulary, which would slip out accidentally at work, as would an occasional literary reference or quote. The guys at the shop started calling me "Einstein" and "Brainiac." There was kidding involved, of course, but at the same time I felt their resentment, as if I were putting on airs—thinking I was better than everyone else. As a result, my love of reading isolated me even more.

One day, as I was sitting with Lupe in my living room, reading a Jules Verne fantasy—me catching the afternoon light by the window and Lupe happily eating a rawhide donut on the floor— I felt more contented than I ever had in my life. I didn't have to drink to relax, or drown out my thoughts with a constant stream of inane television sitcoms. I no longer had to numb my mind to the reality of my unhappy life. Now, I could actually do things that I loved without guilt, shame or fear.

Even so, I was well aware of the fragility of happiness. It had always been so temporary in my life. I now savored each moment of joy, knowing that it could change at any time. I had NOW, and now was very good. My relative peace and joy went on this way for about six beautiful months, but then as I had feared, it was suddenly gone again.

Chapter 6

As I mentioned before, San Sebastian has always been a primarily Mexican-American town, with most residents tracing their ancestry back to the first Spanish settlers in the 1500's. There are some members of the Santa Ana, San Felipe and Sandia Pueblos living there too, and a few Anglos, but it is mostly composed of the Old Spanish "conquistador" families. The ancestors of these folks had spent centuries scratching out hardscrabble lives of subsistence farming. Most everyone in San Sebastian knew each other's history, everyone seemed related in some way, either by blood or marriage, and there was an unspoken loyalty by locals to each other, with a suspicion of strangers, new ideas and of change.

By the time we hit the new millennium, things in San Sebastian had finally started to evolve. There was a housing and population boom in the Albuquerque area as newly arrived Floridians, New Yorkers and Californians abandoned the endless winters of the Northeast, the hurricanes of Florida and the skyrocketing housing costs of California. These newcomers sold their overpriced homes in their respective states and moved to New Mexico, buying spacious new estates with plenty of money left over to spend on high-end restaurants, art galleries, and slot machines. Developers piled into the state like ants on a discarded melon rind, and "faux" adobe houses, made with plywood and cheap stucco, sprang up by the thousands, settling in the sand dunes like flattened tumbleweeds, without even a spindly salt cedar tree for shade.

Soon traffic in the larger metro areas increased and housing prices started to climb. In order to escape the rising cost of Albuquerque and Santa Fe, many outsiders came to San Sebastian because it was still fairly cheap and quite close to the throb of urban life. Some were good people, and some were not.

One of these newcomers bought the house behind me just before my wife died. The family consisted of a rather unsavory looking father, a pale, thin, disheveled mother with sunken eyes, and a bewildered young son. Within a week, screaming and yelling carried over the fence daily, in addition to the sound of shattered glass and broken furniture. The mother and son disappeared within a month after moving in, never to be seen again, and the small house remained inhabited solely by Wendell Pruitt and the assortment of whores, junkies and gang members he befriended.

Needless to say, the immediate neighborhood around Pruitt's house soon became noisy, with loud music blaring long into the night. His yard was filled with trash, old motorcycle engines and beer cans. The simple blue house, previously owned by old man Jaramillo, had been sold by his daughters for almost nothing after he died. What had been a simple, well-kept and cherished home quickly became an eyesore … a blemish on our neighborhood and a nightmare to the community.

I was not home much after Wendell Pruitt moved in, as I was usually working late or drinking out under the bleachers by the baseball field. But Raquel was incensed by this invasion. She called the San Sebastian police several times a week and the officers even went so far as to arrest our neighbor and a few of his friends after the cops found some marijuana there. But, just when our hopes were raised that this despicable man was out of our lives forever, he returned with a fury.

As it turned out, Pruitt's uncle was a well-known businessman in Albuquerque, having built up a chain of discount supermarkets. The uncle bought the friendship of many local and state politicians so he could continue to push his generic stores into developing areas. Out of guilt, loyalty or embarrassment—I'm not sure which—Pruitt's uncle and the high-priced lawyers he hired always managed to keep our miserable neighbor out of jail.

Pruitt hated Raquel, and would toss beer cans over his fence into our yard, make rude whistling noises when she was out hanging up the laundry, alternatively calling her a "bitch" and worse. This just made Raquel even angrier and she would curse back at him in Spanish. Raquel even went so far as to organize a community meeting to discuss the problem, but she died before any plans were put into place to dislodge this parasite.

A short while after Raquel died, I remember sitting alone on the back steps of my house, in mid morning, drinking a beer. As I recall, I was thinking of nothing except wanting to get drunk, when Pruitt made a rare daytime appearance—he was usually stoned or passed out when the sun was shining. He came out his back door, saw me sitting there and went over to the fence and rested his elbows on the edge. He grinned and laughed.

"Sorry about your wife, man. I heard she dropped dead in the back yard." I looked at him, but said nothing.

"C'mon man, you must be relieved! She was a bitch, man. A royal fuckin' bitch. Always in my face. Always makin' trouble. I just want to be left alone, you know. But your fuckin' bitch wife was always mouthin' off, calling the pigs. I hope we don't have no trouble, you and me … "

Pruitt had a cold hard look in his eyes. His thinning brownish hair was disheveled and his pink face blotchy on one side, as if he had just risen from the couch. His words were slurred and hoarse and I guessed he was still drunk. But I especially remember his eyes, framed by dark puffy skin, filled not with just with hate or contempt, but also with a kind of cold hard emptiness.

At that moment, I wanted to get up and smash Pruitt in the head with my beer bottle. Whatever my relationship with Raquel had been, it was unthinkable to allow this animal to say such things about her. I opened my mouth to yell, to scream at him at the top of my lungs, but I couldn't think of anything to say, whispering only "Chinga tu madre" under my breath. I couldn't work up the energy to even stand up and wave my fist. It was as if I didn't exist anymore. I just wanted to be left alone with my beer.

After a minute, Pruitt weaved a little as he tried to remove his arms from the fence top. He squinted his red-rimmed eyes and sneered. I stood up, stared at him for a moment, then turned around and went inside. I remember I drank three more beers and then passed out on the couch, as Oprah Winfrey droned on in the background.

I did not call the police on Pruitt in the coming weeks, despite the noise, the garbage thrown over the fence, the motorcycle engines revving for hours. I did not want to deal with him or the cops … or anyone for that matter. I just wanted to be left alone. And I figured if I left him alone, he would leave me alone.

And he did. Until Lupe came to live with me.

Chapter 7

Lupe's health continued to improve. Her skeletal body filled out and she finally had her cast taken off. Instead of cowering behind the couch every time an ambulance went by or shaking like a leaf at the sound of a backfiring engine, she gradually became more playful and looked forward to taking walks with me. Lupe had evolved from a dog that appeared to be permanently shell-shocked, to a happy canine rummaging through the back yard, digging holes, sniffing at the fence posts and chasing blue-collared lizards. It made me happy to watch her.

We started hiking in the hills and arroyos of Placitas, at the far northern end of the Sandia Mountain. Finding old Indian pottery shards and pieces of petrified wood, Lupe and I would hike silently, enjoying the sound of the wind blowing through the sagebrush and the occasional trill of a Gambel's quail calling his mate. It was at those times that I felt most at peace. The rest of the world seemed a million miles away, yet I did not feel alone.

I think Lupe must have spent a good part of her life in a cage or on a short chain in some trash-filled backyard. I would watch this middle-aged dog become fascinated by every grasshopper, butterfly or praying mantis she discovered, like a puppy let outside for the first time. When a huge jackrabbit would appear nearby, her ears would move from side to side and she would look at me as if to ask "Shouldn't I be chasing that?"

While she was still a bit wary around strange people, Lupe started to warm up to the folks we saw on our walks, her favorite being old Mrs.

Perea, who always carried bone-shaped dog biscuits in her purse. However, like Raquel, Lupe took an immediate dislike to Wendell Pruitt and his friends. Whenever anyone came outside to the neighbor's backyard to either to smoke, drink, throw up or urinate, Lupe would bark furiously. She would go near the fence and bark without respite. If I heard her, I would immediately go out and call her inside. No need to cause trouble with that guy. But, at the same time, I was secretly satisfied that Lupe hated that drunken beast as much as I did, and was willing to offer a protest when I was not.

Pruitt and his pals didn't much like Lupe's barking and would holler out the windows, "Shut that damn dog up! Or "I'm gonna kill that fuckin' dog, if it keeps barking!"

Wine bottles and drinking glasses, and even wrenches and screwdrivers would occasionally soar over the fence, but Lupe would expertly dodge them. I would pick them up later and throw them away. I was ashamed of my cowardice, but, as I said, I didn't want to provoke a war. I just wanted to be left alone. I tried repeatedly to get Lupe to stop barking when Pruitt was around, but she was insistent. She simply hated the man. Maybe he reminded her of other horrible people she had encountered in her life.

Late one afternoon in early April I decided to go to the movies, as it had been such a long time since I had been to one. A feature was playing at the community center, a French movie about the tragic life of French singer Edith Piaf. I was reluctant to leave Lupe alone in the house, but I knew it would only be for a couple of hours. The dog experts on television had said that it was a good idea to leave a dog alone once in awhile—to build confidence, I think they said.

Lupe and I had taken a long walk earlier, and she was happily dozing on the couch, having finished off her dog food. I found out that the movie was only an hour and a half long and I figured I would be back before she even woke up. When I was closing the front door, she looked at me sadly for a moment, but then lay down again and closed her eyes with a big sigh.

The movie turned out to be entertaining, and I was happy that I had done something I hadn't thought of doing for years. I picked up some tortillas and milk at the store, and a box of dog biscuits for Lupe, and then headed home. The sun was starting to set and I was looking forward to a simple dinner and then, maybe, some "Law and Order" reruns on TV. I am embarrassed to say that, even after a couple of hours, I missed Lupe and couldn't wait to see her.

I turned the corner and opened the door to the house, expecting Lupe to come running to me as usual. But nothing happened and the living room was empty. I called Lupe once, then again louder, and then frantically ran around the house screaming her name. I was suddenly in a panic, with the horrible memories of Pepito's disappearance flooding into my head like a tidal wave. I stumbled about, peering under the bed, checking the closets, pleading for Lupe to come out, but I heard nothing but complete silence. I ran to the back door and noticed that it was open. But I had closed it! I know I had. At least, I thought I had. Suddenly, I just couldn't remember.

I sighed and cupped my hand over my rapidly beating heart. I then realized Lupe may have nudged open the screen door, which had then slammed shut, trapped her in the backyard. I went outside smiling and called her. I heard a bark, Lupe's bark I thought, but it seemed a bit distant. Then I heard another bark. Definitely her bark, but muffled somehow. It was more of a yelp. I called her again and walked down the steps into the back yard. It was starting to get dark outside. Maybe she got her collar stuck on a branch near the trees in the far corner. I suddenly panicked. What if her foot had re-broken, or she was being strangled in her own collar, or she had run into a rattlesnake or a scorpion?

I called again, screaming as loudly as I could, and there was a sad whine in response. But it wasn't coming from the trees. It was coming from Wendell Pruitt's yard.

In a panic, my legs like rubber, I stumbled across the yard to the fence, hoarsely crying "Lupe! Lupe!"

I got to the fence and suddenly saw Pruitt, his ugly face dimly lit by a back door light, sitting in his faded green web chair, holding Lupe in his lap. He was tightly grasping her by the scruff of her neck with one hand. In the other hand, he held the point of a large jackknife a few inches from Lupe's outstretched neck. Seeing me, she started to struggle. Lupe tried to move her head and then to bite Pruitt, but his grip was too strong.

I froze. "WHAT … WHAT ARE YOU DOING!?" I hollered, louder than I expected.

"Hey neighbor? Look what I found."

Pruitt was obviously drunk. His eyes looked bloodshot even in the fading light and he was swallowing his words, as if his tongue had grown too thick.

"That is my dog. Let her go right now!"

I was panicked, but also felt the burning fire of rage. I looked at Lupe and she was gasping for breath, her bad leg hanging off the chair. She whimpered, looking at me with wild, terrified eyes. I knew she was pleading for my help.

"Lupe, it'll be alright, girl."

"Lupe, it'll be all right, girl" Pruitt mimicked me. "I wouldn't be so sure Quintana." He pronounced my last name as some Anglos do … "Kwin-tan-a" instead of "Keen-tahna".

Pruitt moved the knife closer to Lupe's throat. "I've told you over and over and over to shut this damn dog up. I sleep during the day, you know, and it really PISSES ME OFF to be woken up by the fuckin' noise!

"I always take her in when she barks, you know that."

"Well, today, she barked and barked for hours, man. I'm telling you, I was ready to explode."

"She got locked out by mistake. I went to a movie."

"Oh, so you go to a movie and leave this bitch behind to bother me and my friends. I quickly glanced behind him and didn't see anyone else around."

"It isn't going to happen again." I said, pleadingly now.

Pruitt laughed … a god-awful, spine-chilling laugh, followed by coughing and finally spitting.

"You're right about that 'Kwin-tan-a.' I'm going to make sure of that!"

He watched me with a widening smile.

I stood there for a moment, stunned. I stared at him. Then at Lupe, who was struggling to breathe. Pruitt tightened his grip on her neck.

"You wouldn't do that," I whispered hoarsely, my heart pounding so loudly I could barely hear myself. "I'll call the police."

"You don't know me very well, do you?" Pruitt's smile faded and he now stared at me with blank olive pit eyes. This man was just empty and evil and cold. I knew he could do it. Hurt Lupe. And I suddenly knew that, if I didn't do something, he **would** do it.

I looked at the fence. It appeared he must have torn off a couple of loose slats and then grabbed Lupe when she went toward him. It looked like she had bitten him on the hand, as there was a wad of toilet paper wrapped around his index finger. Pruitt noticed where I was staring.

"Yeah, man, it bit me too! Fuckin' bitch dog."

He looked at Lupe and then cruelly squeezed her snout. She whimpered and cried and struggled to get away. But his hand was like a vise.

"STOP! You're hurting her" I yelled, but realized it no longer mattered what I said. He wouldn't stop.

I instinctively moved away, toward the house and started running.

"Yeah, call the police," he called after me. "The fuckin' dog BIT me. I'll have killed it in self-defense by the time they get here. No one will care about your ugly ass dog." Then he laughed again.

I ran up the back steps and went right into my bedroom closet where I pulled an old cardboard box from the top shelf. My hands were shaking and I was mumbling something to myself. But I could think only of Lupe out there, terrified, alone with *him.* I had saved her once and she trusted me. She couldn't die. I would not let that happen.

I opened the box and pulled out my gun, a .38 caliber pistol I had bought used when there had been a slew of break-ins on the street about ten years ago. I kept it hidden in the ceiling above the closet and Raquel didn't even know about it. It was fully loaded and I had kept it oiled and in good condition. I would scare the hell out of that creep and get Lupe back.

I ran out of the bedroom and tore as fast as I could down the steps and across the yard, despite my legs feeling as stiff and frail as popsicle sticks. My heart was beating so hard that I started to see black spots in front of my eyes … moving in slow circles. Pruitt was still sitting there, drunk as could be, with Lupe starting to hang limply, her eyes half closed. I knew she was probably suffocating. I had to get her back.

Pruitt looked at my gun first with fear, flinching reflexively, but then, slowly, he relaxed and offered his evil smile.

"You gonna shoot me over a damn dog? What kind of nut are you?"

"I will shoot you if I have to."

"You don't think they'll arrest you? Shooting a man because he tried to defend himself after getting bitten by your vicious dog? And you're too much of a coward, man."

"Let her go!" I yelled.

I moved closer to the fence, raised the gun and aimed it at Pruitt's forehead. He just stared at me with his cold crusted eyes. I knew he wasn't scared of me. I looked again at Lupe … she was barely breathing.

Suddenly, Pruitt raised his knife and pushed the tip against Lupe's neck, staring at me the whole time.

"If you're gonna shoot, man, do it now, cause this bitch is gonna die … "

I remember that what happened next was like a silent movie, in slow motion. Pruitt's arm with the knife angled up to Lupe's throat. He stuck the point into her fur and I jumped when I heard her muffled yelp. I could see a small trickle of blood flow down onto the knife blade.

I suddenly felt an electric jolt tear through my head. Like I was being electrocuted … green and black space illuminated with fireworks of yellow. I don't remember how long it lasted—a second or a minute or an hour. What I remember next, though, was staring at Wendell Pruitt, his head bent strangely to the right, leaning back against the broken green lawn chair. In the middle of his forehead was a bullet hole, with blood trickling down into his hair. It seemed as though everything was suddenly silent … the air felt heavy and still and the last rays of sun reflected ghoulishly on the dead man's colorless face.

I looked down and saw the gun lying on the ground.

Pruitt's hands had slipped off of Lupe and she was lying on the ground, panting. A small amount of blood was running down from her neck, a thin thread of dark red on her tan fur.

I bent down and viciously tore and kicked more slats off of the fence, ducked through and grabbed Lupe, hugging her to my body. A rush of immense relief washed over me when I had her in my arms.

Then I started running. I grabbed a sheet from the laundry line with one hand as I rushed by and pressed it gently against her neck. It was not bleeding very much and it appeared she had only suffered a small puncture wound, made by the knife tip. But I didn't know for sure.

I went to my truck and put Lupe on the seat next to me, gently wrapping her in the sheet. I turned the key in the ignition, my hands now remarkably steady. I drove back to the emergency animal hospital in a blur, not even thinking about which direction I needed to go. My limbs felt very heavy and I had a terrible headache.

I remember hurriedly walking to the front counter of the hospital with Lupe in my arms, pleading for help. By now, Lupe was alert and squirming. The surprised clerk looked at the blood and immediately paged a veterinarian. When they came to take her, I didn't want to let her go and they had to gently pry off my hands. I remember the fear of being alone in the waiting room. I needed to know what was happening. I slumped into a corner seat, with my head in my hands. And I cried as silently as I could. For Lupe. For me. Maybe even a little for Wendall Pruitt.

As it turned out, Lupe was going to be okay. The wound had punctured her skin only about a half-inch and took just two stitches to close. The doctor put in a shunt for drainage because she thought the wound might have gone into Lupe's muscle tissue. They found a kid's t-shirt to put on her to keep her from licking the wound. I slipped it carefully over her, noticing that it said "Besame Mucho" in big blue letters—"***Give me a big kiss***." I still have that blood stained t-shirt. I always will.

I got in the truck to take Lupe home. She was groggy from the anesthetic, shivering a bit, and I covered her with my coat and petted her in long strokes, singing an old Mexican *corrido* to her as we drove down the road.

We passed Our Lady of Guadalupe, maintaining her place in front of the church, and I pulled up to the curb, gazing again at her calm peaceful face peering at the stars. For the first time in years, I prayed. I thanked Guadalupe for saving her namesake, for giving me the strength to rescue my beautiful dog, for allowing me to keep her. When I left, I felt calmer, a sigh escaping my body. For some reason, I wasn't even thinking about what might be awaiting me.

Chapter 8

Wher I drove up to my house, I noticed right away that there were three or four police cruisers parked at the curb, their lights blinking and blazing. Several officers stood talking in a small group on the front lawn. My front door was open, the house lights were on, and the neighbors were crowded together about 50 yards away, whispering to each other.

For a brief moment, I was puzzled by this, my head suddenly foggy and heavy, like it had been magically transformed into a bowling ball. But then, in a moment, I remembered. The confrontation with Pruitt. Lupe being injured. The gun. I shut off the engine and headlights. The cops stopped talking and turned to look in my direction. After hesitating a moment, they drew their weapons and slowly started to march in my direction, instructing me loudly to get out of the truck. I carefully pushed open the driver's door and then lifted up Lupe in my arms, showing the officers that I wasn't holding a weapon. The officers then lowered their guns and I made my way directly into the house through the open door, eyes straight ahead. I half expected a bullet to hit me in the back.

I gently placed Lupe on the couch, watching her sleep for a moment. Then I stood up and turned to face several police who had entered the house behind me. They froze in their tracks. I looked at the figures staring at me and finally said,

"My dog was hurt. I needed to bring her to the vet." They continued to stare wordlessly. Finally, one stepped forward.

"Mr. Quintana. Anastasio Quintana?"

A burly Latino cop looked at me, very tense. I recognized the other two cops in the room, Freddie Montoya and Benny Chavez. I knew them from the street, from church. I had gone to school with Benny's mother. But I didn't know the cop who was asking me questions.

"Yes. I am Anastasio Quintana."

The officers who I knew nodded at me without smiling.

After following their stares, I suddenly realized that I had blood on my shirt and pants, probably on my face as well. It was Lupe's blood, of course. But it looked no different than human blood.

"Do you know why we are here?"

I was silent as I contemplated the question. Finally I said, "I'm not sure."

"Why do you think we're here?"

"Because I had an argument with the neighbor?" I must have sounded quite stupid.

The big cop took another step closer

"What was this argument about?"

I hesitated. Everyone in the room was silent. I could hear Lupe breathing heavily nearby.

I looked him in the eye.

"He took my dog. He was holding a knife to my dog's throat. He was going to KILL her."

I suddenly started to feel my heart pump faster as I recalled what had happened earlier. I broke out into a sweat and felt my hands starting to tremble.

"How did the argument end?" the cop asked brusquely.

"I'm not sure."

"You're not sure?!"

The unfamiliar cop sounded like he was talking to a fibbing child. He glanced at his fellow officers, shaking his head. He then turned back to me.

"How did you get your dog back?"

"He let her go."

"Why did he let her go?"

"Am I under arrest?"

"No. You are not under arrest. Yet. We are just trying to figure out what happened tonight."

"He was trying to kill Lupe."

"Yes, you told us that. But how did you get him to let your dog go?"

"Did I shoot him?" I asked innocently.

There was silence.

I repeated the question. "Did I **shoot** him?"

"Mr. Wendell Pruitt has been shot, yes, Mr. Quintana. We are trying to figure out who shot him and why?"

My voice trembled. "I had to save my dog."

I didn't know what else to say. I felt like I did when I was drunk; confused, spacey, tired. Suddenly, without warning, I started to choke up and let out a big sob. I was embarrassed by this and turned to hide my face. When I had finally stopped crying, I wiped the tears with my sleeve and turned to the burly officer. I started to speak slowly and softly.

"He said he would KILL her … so she would never bark again. I think he was drunk. He had a big knife against her throat. He was serious. About killing my dog!"

"But, he didn't kill your dog. Isn't that your dog there?" The officer pointed to Lupe.

"Yes. But I saved her."

"How?"

I thought for a second.

"I … I … don't know."

The burley cop looked like he had lost his patience. His eyes narrowed and his mouth turned into a sneer.

"Well, sir, it looks like you SHOT Mr. Pruitt. He has a nice big round gunshot wound to his forehead. And we found a .38 caliber revolver on the ground in your backyard."

I stared at him and nodded slightly. I had shot him. I had shot that bastard Pruitt. It didn't seem real because I couldn't remember pulling the trigger. But I must have. It all seemed like one of those exasperating dreams where all the facts are out of order and your mind is drifting back and forth between understanding and confusion. I felt as though someone was telling me a story that I knew was true, but still couldn't quite believe it. I rubbed my eyes and tried to focus again.

"But I saved Lupe," I repeated, glancing over at her sleeping. This appeared to anger the cop.

"Hey, Quintana. Stop looking at the damn dog and look at me." I turned back to him.

"So, you shot and killed the guy, Pruitt, to save a **dog**?" The cop looked at the other cops in mock bewilderment.

"It was self defense!" I yelled. "Look at her. Her neck. All the blood!"

I pointed to my shirt and pants.

"He would have KILLED her. Haven't you been listening to what I've been telling you!?"

Benny Chavez then stepped over to me. Benny's mother and I had been through elementary and middle school together. She never did make it to high school. Benny had been a good son to her, taking her to live in his home with his wife and kids after his father died. He looked at me sympathetically, like he was talking to a senile old man who had wet his pants.

"Don Tacho. It isn't self-defense to save your dog's life. It doesn't matter if the guy WAS trying to kill the dog. But, tell me, was he trying to hurt you too?"

I knew Benny was trying to help me. Everyone knew Pruitt was an evil person, fully capable of trying to kill someone. He probably had succeeded before. And as I look back at Benny's question, I realize that I could have saved myself so much pain if I had responded "Yes."

"No," I replied.

"Did he threaten you personally? Tell you that you were next, anything like that?"

"No."

"Was there someone else there?"

"No. I didn't see anyone else."

"Did he have a weapon?"

"A big knife." I spread my fingers about six inches apart to show them how long the blade was.

"No gun?"

"No. I didn't see one."

"Are you sure?"

I remember being unable to figure out why these cops didn't understand that I did what I had to do. I had to save Lupe, What else COULD I have done? Wouldn't anyone do the same?

"Yes. I'm sure. I didn't see a gun."

The cop produced the gun in a plastic bag.

"Is this **your** gun?"

I looked at it dangling in front of my face.

"It looks like it."

The cops turned from me and there was much whispering. I moved a few feet backward and sat down next to Lupe on the couch, petting her head. I remember I said "Good girl," over and over. She looked peaceful. I wanted to stay here, be with her, and for all these people to leave and the commotion to end. Why was this so hard for them to understand?

Benny came forward, looking very sad, very scared. He licked his dry lips.

"Don Tacho?" I kept petting Lupe and didn't even look up.

"I think she'll be okay," I said softly, more to myself than Benny.

"I'm sorry," Benny said quietly "But we have to arrest you for the murder of Wendell Pruitt. I have to read you your rights.

"Yes, that's okay," I said in a whisper. I still did not look up at him.

Benny read me my rights, but I wasn't listening. I was watching Lupe, lying on the couch sleeping, her ribs rising and falling, rising and falling. I had saved Lupe's life and she had saved mine. We were tied forever to each other.

Finally, Benny said I needed to come down to the police station with them, and the realization dawned that I had to leave Lupe. I panicked. My eyes opened wide and I gasped.

"Oh, no! I can't leave Lupe alone! I have to be here with her. No one else is here!!"

I'm sure I sounded like a senile pathetic fool to them.

The nameless officer said gruffly, "Just take him," but Benny put his hand up.

"Don Tacho, I am calling my wife right now on my cell phone. My wife, Sally? You know we live a few blocks away. I will have her come and take care of your dog. She loves animals and we have a big yard and house. As soon as you come back, we'll bring your dog back to you."

I started pleading. "If I say I don't know who shot him, can I stay?" I know I wasn't making any sense. My head started to throb with dagger-like pulses. Lupe needed me. She trusted me.

"I can't leave her alone … she'll wake up and think I … abandoned her … "

"My wife will be here in ten minutes," Benny said putting a warm hand on my shoulder. "I'll stay with Lupe until then." He patted my back and smiled. The nameless cop rolled his eyes.

I wiped my sleeve across my face. The tears kept rolling down my cheeks. I bent over and kissed Lupe on the top of her head with a tenderness I had never shared with Raquel or Maria, or anyone for that matter. I petted her gently. "I'll be back, Lupita. I promise. Be a good girl."

I was then handcuffed and led toward the door. I looked back at Lupe whose eyes had suddenly opened, looking at me with what appeared to be confusion and fear. But Benny was there with her, talking on his cell phone. As I was walking through the front door, for the first time I heard Lupe howl. It was a pitiful, desperate and mournful sound. If ever there was a time to claim that my heart "broke," it was at that moment. Because that is what it felt like.

I went with the officers and remember little else about that night. They took my fingerprints, tested me for gunpowder residue, took my photo, collected my wallet, but it all seemed like a foggy dream.

The next morning I woke up alone in a jail cell at the Sandoval County jail. It was cold, there was a terrible smell and I was alone. I think I must have passed out from exhaustion once they locked the door. I was still in my clothes, though I didn't have on any shoes or a belt.

My heart started beating wildly again as I remembered that I had been arrested the night before. I stared at the rusted bars of the cell. This couldn't be happening to me. I was always so invisible, so careful to stay out of trouble. And now, suddenly, I was locked up, accused of being a murderer! What would everyone think? My daughter, my friends, the men I had worked with for so many years?

But these disturbing thoughts of becoming a social outcast quickly drifted away once I realized that I had always been one. I started thinking again of Lupe. I knew she was probably all right with Benny and his wife, but I wanted to be with her. I wanted to see her wake up, to feed her, to take her out to the backyard. I wanted her to know that I was still around. And, as I think back, I desperately needed her to let me know that I was still loved.

A door opened up down the hall and I heard approaching footsteps. In a few moments, a large bald man with a drooping mustache came to the bars of my cell and told me that a public defender was assigned to me and I was going to be arraigned that morning. I nodded.

I went quickly to the cell door. "Can you find out how my dog is doing? She was hurt last night."

He smirked at me. "So I understand. I hear someone else was hurt last night as well."

"I know."

"Hey, old man. You KILLED someone last night. Forget about your damn dog."

I sneered at him. "Go fuck yourself."

My head was hurting even more.

"Asshole. You're going to have to get used to this place. And prison is actually a lot worse. Especially for an old shit like you."

Cursing under his breath, the officer took me out of the cell, had me reach my arms behind me and put on handcuffs. He then brought me down a narrow hallway to a small locked room. The room had a dented and peeling metal table and two folding chairs that looked as if they had just been retrieved from the garbage. I sat down and waited in silence for what seemed like hours. That had to be the loneliest room in the world.

Suddenly, a door on the far wall opened and an officer let in a short heavy young woman carrying an oversized briefcase. She looked to be 20 years old, her face pimply and her hair tautly pulled into a ponytail. She was unsmiling, dressed head to toe in black and appeared very nervous.

The woman tentatively reached to shake my hand, but the officer had not taken off my handcuffs. She withdrew her hand quickly, relieved.

"Hello, Mr. Quintana. My name is Sandy Fournier," she began rather woodenly. "I am an attorney with the Sandoval County Public Defender's office who has been assigned to be your attorney for the arraignment today.

The lawyer started rummaging in her briefcase, not even looking at me. She slapped a thin manila folder down on the table and pulled out a pen.

The woman opened the folder, her hand poised above it, still not making eye contact.

"I just need to ask you some questions."

"Why do I need a public defender?" I asked naively.

She looked up and spoke as if she were talking to a toddler.

Because you are going to be A-R-R-A-I-G-N-E-D today. She said the word arraigned loudly and very slowly. That means the judge is going to ask you whether you plead guilty or not guilty to the charges.

"What are the charges?"

"Let's see. The charges include second degree murder, voluntary manslaughter, reckless endangerment, assault with a deadly weapon, unlawful discharge of a weapon … she was reading from the a list in her file.

"I didn't **murder** anyone." Sitting in this horrible room, the fluorescent lights blinking on and off, I was starting to feel sick.

"Mmm hmmm." She kept scanning her papers.

"The police report alleges that you shot and killed a Mr. Wendell Pruitt. Last night, in fact. Now you don't have to tell me whether or not you killed him. We just need to discuss whether you want to plead guilty or non-guilty."

"I didn't murder anyone. It was self defense."

"So we'll plead not guilty." She said this without passion or interest, still doing her best to avoid looking at me.

I watched her write on her pad for a few moments.

"How long have you been a lawyer?"

She looked up, her frozen smile now gone.

"I have a license to practice law in New Mexico."

I nodded. Then sat silently and stared.

She stared back. Hard, challenging, but still fearful. I could see she saw me as nothing but a poor, dumb, dangerous old Latino, who wouldn't hesitate to lunge at her without reason.

"I am perfectly capable of entering a plea for you," she said defensively.

"But you don't seem to care about what happened last night?"

She squinted at me. Her expression looked like a frustrated teenager whose father is reminding her to take out the trash, or to be home by 10 p.m.

She sighed. "What do you want to tell me?"

"Well, I was protecting my dog."

"Yes, I SEE that in the police report."

"This man was going to KILL my dog. He had a knife at her throat. He tried to SLIT HER THROAT!" I expected this revelation to have some effect, but she looked back down at her folder and continued writing.

"Yes, he sounds like quite a disturbed person. But, Mr. Quintana, the law doesn't allow you to kill a person to protect an animal. I mean, you have to remember, it was just a dog."

I thought about this for a minute. I understood what she said and why she said it. I had heard it many times in my life … "Pepito was just a dog, get over it."

I remember once years ago, when I hit a cat with my car, I stopped quickly and tried to see if the cat was all right. We were on the way to the wedding of one of Raquel's many cousins, and she was in a hurry. I remember our conversation well.

"Tacho. Come on. We're going to be late."

"But, I think the cat is still alive. I think it's breathing."

"What are you thinking of doing? Taking it into our car? Getting blood on the seats? Driving it to a hospital!?"

"But, we HAVE to."

"No we don't. Just get in the car. We can't be late. Everyone is waiting for us outside the church."

"You want me to just leave the cat on the street? To die?!"

"It shouldn't have been outside by the road. Maybe someone else will see it."

I remember six-year-old Maria sitting rigidly in the back, her face drained of color, straining to see the poor cat through the rolled-up window.

"What if they don't see it?" I asked Raquel.

Then she said, in an emotionless tone I will never forget, "Oh for God's sakes, Tacho! IT'S JUST A CAT."

I am ashamed to say that I left the cat lying on the side of the road. It may have been dead. I think it was. But I could have sworn I saw it breathe. I thought of nothing else during the wedding and reception and as soon as it was over, I quickly drove back past the scene. The cat was gone, but I could see bits of hair and blood in the gutter. I said nothing to Raquel when we got home, but went to the back yard and quickly drank a six-pack of beer.

I now looked hard at the public defender. Why was she so stupid? What did she know about me? About Lupe? How could I have a lawyer who wouldn't LISTEN to me. My anger started to build.

"Lupe is my dog!! She is … mi familia, my family!!!" I yelled much too loudly.

And then, I was shouting ever louder,

"She was only barking. Dogs bark. But HE TRIED TO KILL HER!!!! What the hell was I supposed to do, sit there and *watch*?! Watch that bastard KILL Lupe?!"

I stood up quickly, but without being able to steady myself with my arms handcuffed behind me, I swayed from side to side trying to regain my balance. I know I must have looked like a bug-eyed lunatic.

A look of panic suddenly filled Sandy Fournier's eyes, and she moved backwards toward the door, hastily stuffing her papers into her briefcase. She banged on the door from which she had entered like she was being pursued by an approaching zombie. The officer finally opened it, and the lawyer turned to me.

"I think you'll need to get another lawyer." And with that, the door slammed shut and she was gone.

Chapter 9

I sat alone in my cell for the eternity that stretched until 2 p.m. I could hear coughing, a radio and some periodic screaming in the nearby cells, but otherwise it was quiet. I felt terrible—exhausted, confused, hungry and in need of a shower. I hadn't eaten the breakfast they had served and was feeling queasy from an empty stomach. I kept thinking back to the events that brought me to this squalid jail cell, trying to make sense of it all. I remembered most of what had happened in a hazy ill-defined way. I knew I had grabbed my gun, that I had run across the yard as fast as I could. I recalled that, after I saw Lupe being stabbed by Pruitt, I had felt a rush of heat flood in my head and saw a bright flash of light. And I knew that Wendell Pruitt was dead. That I had killed a man. Yet, any feelings of guilt and remorse never came. At the time, I could honestly say that I felt no regret.

With my mind drifting back and forth, from past to present and back again, the one thread that stayed in my mind was the thought of Lupe. I knew that Benny would take care of her … promises to a fellow community member are not taken lightly in San Sebastian. One could easily become forever stained with the reputation of being "unreliable." But, even so, I wanted to be with her. I wanted to comfort her. I guess I needed her to comfort me.

Suddenly, a deputy appeared at my cell door. I hadn't even heard the footsteps.

"Hands behind you," he said in a monotone. No, "please," or "I need to ask you … " I was no longer quiet agreeable Don Tacho, but just a crazy old killer.

I was marched handcuffed down the hall, the other prisoners watching me silently from their cells, and then brought to a waiting van. I sat on a bench across from two other men, both younger, with shaved heads, tattoos and cold eyes. They glanced at me, and then looked out the window, never bothering to turn in my direction again.

When we got to the Courthouse, I was marched to the back door, while people in the parking lot watched keenly. I started to feel ashamed and embarrassed. My parents, my poor dead wife, and my daughter would be horrified if they saw me now, though perhaps not surprised. After all, I had never really been an object of pride to anyone. But, once again, I thought of Lupe, and these negative thoughts drifted off. I did what I had to do, I told myself. What any sensible person would do. The judge would understand that. It was so clear to me at the time.

I waited in a small room and when it was finally my turn to be arraigned, a door opened and a deputy came and brought me inside. I was behind a four-foot wall, but I could see that the courtroom was packed with people. All of them turned their eyes to me and I felt paralyzed with shame. I realized that I would probably see people around the courtroom that I knew, so I fixed my stare at the judge's bench. I didn't even check to see whether Sandy Fournier was around.

It was then I saw a thin man of medium height, closely set eyes, a full head of short dark hair and small wire-framed glasses. He was leaning over to speak to the judge's clerk. The clerk then turned and looked at me, pointing. The man glanced over to me and quickly approached with a smile on his face. He extended his hand.

"Mr. Quintana? Hi, My name is David Rubin. I am an attorney in Albuquerque who was a classmate of your daughter Maria … we both attended UNM undergrad together."

He waited for a moment for this to register. I said nothing.

"Well, anyway, Maria called me this morning and asked me if I would agree to represent you. If that is okay with you, of course. At this stage, all we need to do is enter a plea of not guilty and try to get bail set."

The lawyer spoke quickly, loudly and assertively, suggesting to me that he was not native to New Mexico. Folks raised here are usually more soft-spoken and quiet and no one ever seems in a rush to finish a sentence.

I know I probably looked old and confused. I was embarrassed that my clothes were wrinkled and I probably smelled like overripe fruit.

Then it suddenly occurred to me, "Maria?! I'm sorry. How did she find out about this?

But then I knew. Of course. By now, everyone in San Sebastian probably understood more about what happened yesterday than I did. In this town, gossip spreads more quickly than a Bosque fire in August. Maybe Benny called her. Maybe the jail. Sandy Fournier? But now Maria knew. A heavy sadness suddenly hung over me.

David leaned toward me with a tight smile. He seemed to understand my embarrassment at involving my daughter in this mess.

"Mr. Quintana, Maria is worried about you. She told me to tell you that she will be flying down today from Seattle. She has already wired money to post bail, and I think we can get Judge Lujan to keep it at a reasonable level. Look, you have lived in San Sebastian all your life, never been arrested … "

I had seen many legal shows on television over the years. Yet, I felt as though this was all being spoken in a foreign language. Bail. I needed to be bailed out. I had to enter a plea … I had gone from watching a movie yesterday at this time to standing disheveled, starving, in a crowded courtroom, waiting to enter a plea in a murder case and be granted bail …

I nodded at the lawyer and tried to smile. He must be pitying his poor friend Maria for having such a troublesome father. But I wasn't going to turn his help away. I would pay Maria back as soon as I could.

"Thank you … Mr. Rubin. I appreciate your help."

"I don't know if it would make you feel uncomfortable, but why don't you just call me David. We need to get to know each other pretty quickly and it's a lot easier." He smiled again and nodded his head.

The arraignment was fairly quick and I didn't say a thing. The case was called. The judge asked for a plea. David entered a plea of not guilty, talked about my ties to the community, my age, my spotless record and the bail was set at $5,000 cash bail, or $50,000 bond. I couldn't bear to have Maria spend all that money on me, but I said nothing and I was brought back to the jail, where I was eventually "processed" and released.

David had arranged to meet me outside the jail, so he could drive me home. When I left the building, I saw him standing at the bottom of the stairs by a shiny white Saab convertible. But after I had descended the stairs, we started walking further down the street to a beat up old Ford wagon, covered with dust. He saw my face, and laughed.

The Saab belongs to the judge. I have five dogs, so I need this old tin can." He patted his car affectionately.

We drove the two miles home quickly and I was so tired I could barely talk, but I thanked David and promised to come to his office in Albuquerque in a couple of days to discuss the case. He told me to get some rest, adding that he was looking forward to seeing Maria again after so many years. I smiled and nodded. I, on the other hand, was terrified of seeing her.

Chapter 10

When I got inside my house, I found a note on the kitchen counter with Benny's telephone number. I quickly called and reached his wife Sally, who told me that she would bring Lupe back within a half-hour. Apparently, the DA's office had wanted to keep Lupe impounded at the county shelter as evidence in my criminal case, but Benny had been able to convince them that Lupe would be fine with me. As one would expect in this town, Benny is the cousin of one of the judge's clerks and was able to pull some strings. That is how things are done in San Sebastian. I thanked Sally profusely and then sat on the front steps waiting for Lupe to get home.

When the car finally pulled up at the curb, and Sally opened the passenger door, I watched as Lupe leapt from the car and made a mad dash toward me. Her mismatched ears were flopping in different directions and her tongue was hanging out the side of her mouth like a folded tortilla. My heart suddenly flooded with excitement and I hugged Lupe as hard as I could without hurting her. She licked my face a few times and then stared at me with a look of such wide-eyed joy, I completed melted. I patted her head and watched as she ran up the steps to check out her food dish. The world was as it should be again in Lupe's mind.

I thanked Sally again. She kissed my cheek and whispered in my ear, "Hang in there, Don Tacho. I believe in you." Those were probably the last kind words I was to hear from a neighbor for a very long time.

Later in the afternoon, when the sun started to lose its glare and intensity, I took Lupe out for a walk on El Camino de Pueblo, a quiet street lined on either side by a column of thick-limbed cottonwood trees. It was good to be back home with Lupe, but I also had a heavy heart knowing what lay ahead for me.

As we walked, I noticed that people on either side of the street were avoiding me and turning onto side streets, into stores and back into their homes before I reached them. I saw faces peering out of windows and children on bikes stopping suddenly, pointing in my direction and whispering to each other. I had foolishly assumed that, once I got home again, everything would continue as normal. But, I suppose, the sudden discomfort of my neighbors wasn't all that surprising given I was now accused of being a murderer. I doubt anyone in town harbored any sadness over the death of Wendell Pruitt, but these were simple people, with routine lives. Being around someone who killed a man over a dog was not something they were prepared to handle.

Lupe and I headed home eventually. The setting sun was turning the Sandia into a soft pink slice of watermelon and the shadows were dark and deep. Lupe was sniffing trees, periodically looking to me with that crazy huge dog-grin, proudly wearing her clean wrinkle-free Besame Mucho t-shirt. I guess Sally must have washed and ironed it, bless her heart.

When we turned onto our street, I noticed an unfamiliar car in front of the house and the light on in the living room. Curiously and cautiously, I walked up the steps. Suddenly the door opened, and Maria stood there looking at me with a forced smile.

"Hello, Papi. I hope you don't mind. No one was at home and the back door was open, like always."

I shook my head, "No," standing there for a moment unable to think of what to say. Maria reached out and hugged me awkwardly and, just as I was raising my arms to put around her, she quickly stepped back.

Maria was uncomfortable and nervous, like a woman forced to deal with a friend's terminal illness.

"Okay Papi. Come in and rest. Wait, Is this Lupe, the dog I've heard so much about?"

Maria crouched and reached over to pet Lupe. Lupe backed up a few steps, her ears folded back, unsure of this stranger. Maria had always loved animals, despite her mother's hatred of them, and she sat down on the top step, carefully offering Lupe her outstretched hand. Lupe slowly approached Maria and sniffed her fingers. After a few moments, Lupe came close enough for Maria to scratch the top of her head. A sponge for any type of affection, Lupe decisively concluded that Maria was not a dog-beater or knife-wielding maniac, and happily followed her into the house.

I was dreading this moment. This conversation. My poor daughter now had to deal with the fact that her neglectful drunken father was accused of being a murderer too. I had been happy that Maria had found a new life in Seattle, that she had friends and a career. I missed her, but was happy that she rarely came home. I just couldn't bear the uneasy feeling of forever disappointing her.

We sat down at the Formica kitchen table that had been a fixture in the room since Maria was a baby. She ran her finger along the chrome edging, as if remembering her many meals there.

"You didn't need to come, Mija," I said softly, looking down at the table as I said this.

"No. No. You're wrong Papi," she said softly. "Of course I had to come." She said this quietly and without conviction.

I looked up.

"But this isn't something that you should have to deal with. I created this problem by myself ... as usual. You have responsibilities in Seattle. I can handle this ... really."

Maria shook her head stubbornly.

"I took my vacation leave from work ... I have 12 weeks saved and my boss is very understanding. It's not a problem. My neighbor is going to take care of my cat. I can help you while ... you know ... this thing goes on."

I rested my head on my hand. I suddenly wanted a beer very badly. This was always how I felt when I wanted to hug and kiss my daughter and tell her how much I loved her and needed her. I wanted to drink, so I could forget all the guilt and shame and be relieved again to be alone. I looked up, my eyes blurred with tears.

Maria didn't say anything or touch me. She suddenly stood, backed up and leaned against the counter with her arms crossed. She looked at me with a strange expression; not of concern, but of pity, I thought, or maybe contempt. I could almost hear her thoughts, "What am I going to do with this bastard?"

I quickly dried my eyes with my sleeve and excused myself. I was horribly tired, weak and confused. I could feel Maria's eyes following me as I left the room. Lupe stood in the doorway, not knowing whether to follow me or stay with Maria. When I reached my bedroom, I found Lupe was beside me. I lay down on the bed, closed my eyes and was fast asleep within a minute.

Chapter 11

When I woke up early the next morning, I could smell the wonderful enticing aroma of fresh coffee. Maria! It dawned on me that my daughter was back. I quickly took a shower, dressed in some of my nicer clothes, and went to the kitchen.

"Good morning, Papi." Maria said with a somewhat forced grin. Did you sleep well?

"Yes, I did, thank you."

We sounded so stiff and uncomfortable, like two acquaintances passing each other on a crowded bus. Lupe ran into the room, panting, her tail sweeping the air.

"Hello sweet thing," Maria said, petting the dog. This time, her smile was genuine.

Maria busied herself making toast and scrambled eggs. Finally, she sat down across from me and we stared at each other for a moment.

I looked down at my plate and said softly, "Thank you for coming, Maria. Thank you, so much, miha."

Maria rested her head on her palm and nodded.

In silence, I ate and she sipped coffee for what seemed like forever. Lupe busied herself sniffing the garbage.

Finally Maria spoke.

"So. Papi. What happened?"

Maria was staring at me, expressionless, her dark eyes boring into mine. At 40 years old, she still looked like a woman barely out of her twenties, very pretty with smooth cinnamon-colored skin, long black hair in a ponytail, jeans and a white t-shirt. At 5'9", she had taken after me in height, towering over her cousins since she was 15.

Maria had been blessed with good looks, despite the fact that both her parents were rather ordinary looking. But, instead of being grateful, Maria saw this as a curse. As a child, she had always been uncomfortable with compliments about her looks and took pains to dress in drab clothes, wear no makeup and keep her hair short. Maria rebuffed any boy in school who she thought did not respect her intelligence, and the pretty girls at school who invited her into their elite cliques were always taken aback by Maria's cold rejection. Heaven help the person who innocently suggested that she become a model.

Today, I noticed that she had dusky circles under her eyes.

I coughed, put down my coffee and looked at my hands.

"It was for her," I said, jerking my head toward Lupe. He … the neighbor, who your mother hated so much, was going to kill her."

There was a moment of silence. Then Maria touched my hand.

"Tell me."

I started explaining what had happened that terrible afternoon, talking faster, getting more excited and then upset. Maria knew some about how her mother felt about Wendell Pruitt, and now I told her the terrible things he had said about Raquel.

"So, he was going to kill Lupe. I must have shot him."

Maria looked confused.

"What do you mean? Must have … Don't you remember … shooting him?"

"I … remember pointing the gun. And then I remember … seeing him sitting there … not moving. I don't … I mean, of course I shot him. But, I can't remember actually pulling the trigger."

"Did you explain all this to the police. The things he said. What he threatened to do?"

"Yes. They kept telling me you cannot kill a man to save the life of … a dog."

"Did you talk about this to David? Did you explain it? Papi, it wasn't your fault. He started it."

Maria had always had a quick temper, becoming angry about anything she saw as unjust or unfair, and her voice started to get louder, her face reddening.

"We haven't really talked yet. But we are going to meet soon."

Without realizing what I was doing, I took Maria's hand and looked her in the eye. "I am so sorry."

Maria looked startled and then embarrassed, gently patting the back of my hand and withdrawing hers. She started to clean the table, then turned to wash the dishes. She couldn't look me in the eye. Once again, I felt ashamed.

"David is a very good lawyer, Papi. He will know what to do."

"Yes. He seems very smart. Very nice."

I wanted to ask Maria so many questions. "Where did she get the money for the bail? Did she think I was a murderer? Was I a foolish old man defending a dog? Why did she come in the first place? How long could she stay?"

I needed Maria to be with me, yet wanted her to go away. I hated having this conflicted feeling again. The belief that, no matter what I did or said, I could never be anything but a disappointment, a failure and a fool. But, at the same time, I had never stopped hoping she could love me somehow.

"I have to take Lupe for a walk. Would you like to go?"

I could tell Maria was about to say no. I imagined she did not relish walking around her hometown with her drunken old father, who was now a murderer too, together with the infamous mongrel who spurred the killing. I think she would have hated the pity more than the contempt.

She dried her hands with a towel and, to my surprise, said "Yes. Let's go for a walk."

I offered a tight nervous smile and put Lupe's leash on. I found out from Sally that the judge had ordered that Lupe be leashed and under my control at all times, due to her "dangerousness." The law saw her differently than I did, I guess.

Maria and I walked down our street and she commented on what had changed … a new roof on the Garcia house, the Pereas no longer had their old adobe garage, there was a new neon sign at the feed store … I offered up all the local gossip, and we occasionally laughed. Especially at the story of old senile Celia Gutierrez running through the annual Mattachines parade, wearing only a pair of long silk gloves.

We passed people on the street and they said hello to Maria, but avoided making eye contact with me. Maria was polite but distant. As a private person, I think she had always found the gossipy tendencies of the townspeople to be suffocating. I think that is one of the reasons she had left for Seattle so quickly after finishing college.

I tried to ignore the cold stares and the pitying clucks. I focused on Lupe and Maria, on our walk … a walk I could never have imagined just last week. Soon we were home again.

Lupe had some water and went to take a nap on my bed. I didn't know what else to do, so I sat on the couch.

There was so much to say to Maria that I had never had a chance to explain. I wanted to tell her how much I loved her when she was little and how I had wanted her to be happy. Long ago, I had come to the realization that Maria had been trapped between a cold angry mother and a passive, drunken father. She had to be satisfied with just surviving. How does one make right so many wrongs of the past? Maybe it was just not possible.

"I'm going to go to the store for some food, Papi. I'll be back later."

Maria left and I was alone. I suddenly felt a wave of exhaustion and sadness, a familiar misery I hadn't felt since before I had met Lupe. I had been able to live each day without disappointing my dog. I couldn't get such a pass from my daughter.

I went to the bedroom and lay down next to Lupe who sighed and put her head across my chest. I stared at the ceiling and tried to feel remorse for what I had done to Wendell Pruitt. Wouldn't a sane and good man be ashamed and guilty having killed another person? Shouldn't I be crying and gnashing my teeth, going to confession every morning and praying for my redemption? I should be. That's what a decent person would do. But I didn't feel regret, remorse or guilt. Nothing. I realized that no matter how many sorrows I had about my life, I just wasn't ashamed or sad at what I had done. I had acted out of love, I had acted to save another life. A dog's life, I know … "just a dog." But she was my dog and I loved her. I guessed I was damned for eternity. Yet, at least for the time being, I wouldn't be lonely and neither would Lupe.

Chapter 12

The days drifted by, a stilted formality continuing between Maria and me. She stayed for a few more days and then, when she had no more cleaning or shopping to do, she decided to temporarily go back to Seattle. We had chatted uncomfortably in the period before she left, but just superficial stuff. Weather, local politics, Lupe of course. I still longed to talk to Maria about her life away from San Sebastian, of which I knew little. I wanted to offer her advice and let her lean on me for support, like other fathers do with their daughters. But I didn't know how. I never had.

I remember one time Raquel dragged me to one of Maria's clarinet recitals at her middle school, despite the fact that I had already drunk a six pack of beer. One after the other, I watched Maria's classmates choking the life out of their clarinets; squeaking, honking and painfully laboring through their unrecognizable songs. When Maria's turn came, I prepared myself for more of the same, but my daughter resolutely marched to center stage and played the theme song of "The Sting," loudly and beautifully. At the end of the performance, the principal came up to Raquel and me and asked me, "So, Mr. Quintana. What do you think of your talented daughter?!" Maria stood next to her mother, staring at me quietly with a mixture of curiosity and desperation. I suddenly felt tongue-tied, dizzy and confused. Uncomfortable seconds ticked by and my mouth failed to formulate any response. Finally, Maria turned around and ran across the auditorium. It was only then that I was able to whisper, "She was wonderful."

I went to see David at his office in Albuquerque the day Maria was to leave for Seattle. Though I wanted to ask David if I could bring Lupe with me, I decided not to be presumptuous or rude and left Lupe at home. It was a beautiful day, blue sky and cloudless, but I felt nothing but gloom. I would have greatly preferred the sky to be filled with gray rumbling clouds and crackling thunder, more aptly suiting my desperate situation. I was starting to realize that I was probably going to prison. I didn't know what this lawyer could possibly do to save me.

David's office was in a two-story building off of Central Avenue in downtown Albuquerque. It was concrete and spare and I saw he shared the building with a realtor and someone who offered "Reiki," whatever that is. When I entered the office of David Rubin and Associates, there was a chunky middle-aged Latina at the front desk, eating a candy bar and reading the newspaper.

"Hi. I'm here to see Mr. Rubin."

The woman looked up, put down her candy bar, and smiled.

"Hello, Mr. Quintana. I'm Elsie Reyes. I'm the one who actually runs this office, and don't let David tell you otherwise. I bet I could handle most of these cases myself, after all that I've seen and done here. I mean, we just had a man last week who was accidentally hit by a car in Old Town, and it turns out the car was driven by his sister-in-law! I told him to just try to work it out so there wouldn't be any family problems, you know what I mean. I'm sure David wouldn't be happy to hear that I had turned away business … "

Elsie was what I call a "chimosa." This Spanish word denotes someone who is a gossip; who is loud, verbose, vulgar and grandiose. Since I am generally such a quiet man, I usually say nothing with such people, just listen. The chimosa's energy usually burns out without someone stoking the fire. When I just smiled and did not respond, Elsie soon sat down and pointed to one of the three mismatched chairs in the waiting room.

"Okay then. I'll tell David you're here."

David came right out and ushered me into his office. It was nothing like the television shows where the criminal defense attorney has a brilliant view of the mountains, a row of law books floor to ceiling and a highly polished maple desk the size of a small room. This space had the disheveled look of a San Sebastian High School guidance counselor's office. David had books open on his desk, papers piled up a foot high on the floor. I wondered whether someone this disorganized would be able to help me. But then, I figured, I didn't really have the money or the connections to be too choosy. Besides, my daughter said he was good, and that sat well with me.

We chitchatted politely for a few minutes—New Mexicans rarely just launch into business without some preliminary pleasantries. "How are Maria and Lupe?" "Did you hear that a storm is coming?" "What was all that about the Governor having a boating accident at Elephant Butte?" Finally, David sat down across from me and became serious.

"Mr. Quintana. Anastasio. I have to tell you, this is a very troubling case. We have you confessing to killing Mr. Wendell Pruitt with your own gun, from your own yard, when he was armed with only a bowie knife. It appears that Pruitt was too far away to threaten any real harm to you, and I don't think we could honestly argue that you were worried he was going to throw the knife at you. From what I've read in the police report, I'm also going to assume for now that you weren't coerced into giving a confession."

I thought for a moment.

"No I wasn't," I replied.

"Now, I need to have access to your medical records, so we can see whether you have been suffering from any illness that may have caused … I don't know … confusion."

"Confusion?"

"You know, pain medications can make you groggy and disoriented, some antidepressants can put you into a kind of trance, and other medications have been known to cause walking blackouts … "

"I am not taking any medications. I haven't been to the doctor in years."

He looked at me sadly. "Oh, I see." He tented his fingers under his chin.

"Have you been having any problems with your health?"

"No, not really. I recently stopped drinking and went through the DT's. I feel much better now."

He suddenly bolted up in his chair.

"Yes, that is worth exploring. People often have hallucinations and paranoia when withdrawing from alcohol."

I saw where he was going. While that type of defense could be my salvation, something inside me told me I couldn't lie about this. About what really happened.

"Well, I stopped drinking many weeks before the … thing … with Wendell Pruitt. I had felt fine for quite awhile."

Again, David looked deflated.

"Well, Mr. Quintana. Let's do this. Why don't you tell me in your own words what happened that night. I want you to know that I will represent you no matter what you tell me, and nothing you say ever leaves this room. Not even to Maria. So just tell me what you believe happened that afternoon."

I sighed and looked down at my fingernails. I so much did not want to talk about this. But I nodded and looked up.

"It was actually very simple. That man … took Lupe, was choking her, cut her with his knife and was going to kill her. I needed to save her."

"Okay. Go on."

"Well, I knew that look in Pruitt's eyes. I've seen it before. People I know who have beaten their wives or children, who provoke fights, who kill animals for fun. It was a cold, almost empty stare. And I knew then that Pruitt was going to kill Lupe. That he was actually looking forward to it. And that he couldn't wait to see my reaction once he did it. I saw it in his eyes."

"What else did you try to do to get him to let go of the dog?"

I sat silently for a moment and felt an empty hole in my stomach recalling that horrible evening.

"I'm not ashamed to say that I begged him. I pleaded with him. I threatened him. I told him that I was going to call the police. But he thought it was all funny. He didn't care about how I felt or how much I pleaded for my dog's life. He didn't care about the police. He WANTED to kill Lupe."

"I realize that must have been a terrible realization, Mr. Quintana. But what made you go back to the house to get a gun? Were you going to use it to threaten him?"

"I don't know. I just knew I had to do something to get my dog back."

There was silence for a moment as I got a little choked up. I usually keep my emotions tightly secreted away, but remembering the terrified expression on Lupe's face, my complete helplessness, was making me feel increasingly ill.

"Well, maybe you didn't mean to fire the gun. Was it an accident? Do you know how to shoot a gun?"

"Yes."

"Maybe you were under such stress you blacked out. The police report says that you told the officers at the scene that you didn't remember shooting him."

"Well, I realized it afterwards. I saw the gun on the ground. I saw him slumped over … with … all that blood. His blood … and Lupe's blood."

"But you don't remember the exact moment shooting him. Pulling the trigger, watching the bullet hit him?"

"No. I don't know why. I just don't remember it. I remember standing there pointing the gun, seeing him put the knife in her neck, and then nothing until I saw him leaning back in his chair. Already dead."

David sat and looked at me, thinking silently to himself. I didn't speak. Finally, he leaned over toward me.

"Anastasio. What we need to do is have you see a forensic psychiatrist. I have worked with her for many years and she is excellent. She needs to talk to you about all this."

A psychiatrist? I was stunned. I mean, I understand that many people see psychiatrists and I have even read a little Freud and Jung at the library, but I felt immediately embarrassed and ashamed. Was I crazy as well as weak? What would my daughter think?

"Why?" I said finally.

"You have to understand. The law in New Mexico, or anywhere for that matter, does not allow a person to kill another person EXCEPT in self-defense or defense of "another." But defense of another does not include animals, even a family dog. It doesn't matter how cruel someone is being to an animal, even one you own. You can't kill that person to stop it."

I shook my head.

"You mean, I should have let him slit her throat as she looked at me standing there, doing nothing?" I was incredulous. Of course, now I know the law, but it just seemed ridiculous to me at the time.

David nodded sympathetically. "Go on."

"I couldn't let him kill her. How could I live with myself afterwards?"

As I thought about it, I realized this wasn't just a turn of phrase. I actually didn't think I could have lived with myself and that memory of Lupe dying, looking at me with her pleading eyes. I don't think I would have allowed myself to continue with that image in my head.

I looked at David, my voice firmer. Suddenly, I wanted him to understand me.

"But, I asked him to give Lupe back. He had a choice and he refused to do the right thing. How could the law say that it isn't okay to save her LIFE. Are animals just worthless?"

"No of course not, Anastasio. But the law is the law, whether or not you or I like it. However, these are important issues that the psychiatrist will discuss with you. Perhaps you didn't make the critical distinction between dog and human when it came to Lupe. Maybe you over-identified with her, became too confused or overwhelmed by your emotions. You know, what was in your mind the moment you pulled the trigger? We need to know all this to put on a defense."

I nodded. No more arguing. I would leave the case in his hands. But, deep down, I still knew that I had done the right thing and would not allow a psychiatrist to force me to say otherwise.

I went home, quickly scooting out the waiting room door to avoid another longwinded speech from Elsie Reyes.

Maybe the world was wrong, the law was wrong … it seemed so to me at the time. But then, I thought, Anatasio Quintana is not going to be the one who changes the law or the way the world thinks. I guess I needed to get used to the idea now that I was simply a confused, crazy old man who loved his dog more than his fellow human beings. People, after all, had never really given me any love. But Lupe had.

I knew deep down that, no matter what anyone said to describe my state of mind or motivations, I had no regret that Lupe was alive and Wendell Pruitt was dead. Did that make me a soulless killer, a demented maniac? Maybe in the eyes of the law. But in my own eyes, I was finally proud of standing up for something. For someone.

I suddenly had the urge to see Lupe. And I was relieved that Maria would not be at home.

Chapter 13

To my surprise, when I got home, Maria WAS there, washing the floors. Lupe was on the couch, happily panting, and I stood there with a look of shock on my face.

Maria looked up without smiling.

"These floors are really yellow and dirty. A little scrubbing and wax and look at how wonderful they are."

I didn't see much change, but I admired it nevertheless.

"I just have to finish this corner," she said, back to mopping.

"Why are you here?" I finally said. "I thought you had gone home this morning." Maria put down the mop and wiped her forehead.

"Well, when I finished packing, I was sitting on the couch with Lupe and realized that I didn't have any really strong reason to be in Seattle instead of here ... I mean, I live alone. My cat is at the neighbor's most of the time anyway. I'm actually very burned out at my job. So, I called up my boss and took an extended leave of absence from work, turned the cat over to my neighbor and gave my houseplants to my friend Paula. She has always wanted my Sego palm tree."

I looked at her. Before I could stop myself, I asked, "But, WHY?"

Maria blushed and looked away. She returned to mopping.

Quietly, between strokes, she said, "I thought ... maybe ... you needed me."

Before waiting for a response, she and her mop moved into the kitchen.

I gave Lupe a big hug and she jumped down from the couch and went with me to the backyard. Suddenly, I realized that Maria had not made Lupe get off the couch, like her mother would certainly have done. This made me smile.

Lupe stood in the middle of the yard, facing me, tail wagging furiously, mouth open and panting with a fixed look in her dark eyes. Her ears, as always, drooped in different directions. She looked at me with such unabashed joy, anticipation, and contentment, I felt moved to kiss her head. Why did she make me feel like I was worth something? That I really mattered? Shouldn't only people have that power?

Maria came out to the back steps and sat down with a cup of tea.

"How did the meeting with David go?"

I didn't really want to talk about it, but sat down next to Maria and explained what had happened. That I was going to see a psychiatrist. That he didn't want me to worry about his legal fee, he wanted to handle my case as a favor to Maria.

Maria said nothing but nodded solemnly.

I caught her glancing at me with what looked like sympathy and sadness, but she turned away immediately. She patted my shoulder and then quickly went into the house.

Later, we sat and watched television silently, Lupe on the couch with me, and Maria in the torn recliner. We watched a cable nature program on what happens to a forest after a fire rages through it ... what dies and what grows in its place. One fascinating segment was about a tree called the "Manzanita." Apparently, some species of this tree drop their seeds onto the forest floor, but the seeds do not germinate or grow unless they are first scorched by a fire. Amazingly, these seeds sit patiently on the forest floor, perhaps for decades, waiting for a blazing fire to melt their tough shells and to stimulate their growth cycle. I am just stunned by nature sometimes.

I looked over at Lupe, who had dropped her head into my lap and was sleeping, a few leg jerks now and then and soft moans. I hoped that she wasn't having nightmares, horrifying dreams of past torment. While neither of us could control our dreams, at least now we could always wake up to something better.

A few days later, I met with the psychiatrist hired by David. Her office was in Rio Rancho, a sprawling suburban city built on sand dunes and connected to Albuquerque like mismatched jigsaw puzzle pieces you pound together with your fist. All the buildings looked alike to me … mini-strip malls and houses three feet apart from one another. Everything appeared square, two stories and stucco'ed, with sad-looking yuccas planted here and there. The office was off of the main highway, in a small building sitting beside a Walgreens drugstore. This certainly did not look like what I had expected from a psychiatrist's office. No prime time television shrink would ever treat patients in such a mundane setting.

I was filled with dread at this visit. I had never seen a psychiatrist. I had never wanted my thoughts to be probed by a stranger, knowing that I would inevitably be considered incurable and crazy, or at least hopeless. I had always been taught by my parents that, whatever your inner demons, they belong hidden from view as they were of no interest to anyone else. No matter how desperate or unhappy you were, you went on acting as normal as possible, because your family name required it, your children depended on it, and the Church demanded it. That is why so many people I grew up with turned to alcohol and drugs as a way of coping with death, divorce, depression and loneliness.

I was ushered into the doctor's office and was quickly face to face with a slim dark-haired woman, about 40 or 45 years old, with no makeup and dressed casually in a short sleeve shirt and khaki slacks. I was directed to sit in a chair across from her, and she sat several feet away, facing me. I had expected someone quite commanding and cold, with a thick pad of paper, pursed lips and half-moon bifocals clasping the tip of her nose. In fact, she seemed like someone I might bump into at the San Sebastian grocery store.

"Hello Mr. Quintana. I am Dr. Melanie Ortiz, and I was hired by your attorney to do a forensic examination. What that means is that I am going to ask you some questions about your life, your upbringing, your family and the like, and also about the events that led to your present criminal charges. I'm not here to judge you or to label you. I just want to **understand** you. So, relax and don't be afraid to tell me what is on your mind. I must tell you that this consultation is not meant to be strictly confidential since it is going to be shared with your attorney. But, if Mr. Rubin does not wish to use anything from my report in your case, or you don't want him to, no one else will ever have access to it.

She smiled and nodded. "Do you understand, Mr. Quintana?"

"Yes."

I sat silently, wondering whether I would be able to talk freely to a stranger about my family, my failings and my tormented life. These were always such private thoughts, and I had spent enormous energy keeping them secret. But I would try.

During the interview, we talked about my childhood, about my mother and father. I started by telling the doctor how hardworking and pious my parents were, but she encouraged me to tell her what I thought about them and how they behaved, not how the community saw them or how they presented themselves. For some reason, I felt safe with Dr. Ortiz. And the terrible memories, locked safely away for so long, started tumbling out like water coursing down a flooded arroyo.

I told her about the beatings, the drinking, the fights, the incident with Pepito. I explained about how living with Raquel, while not violent, was really no different than being with my parents ... she was judgmental, tyrannical and angry. I told the doctor about my alcoholism, about my fear of disappointing Maria, about how I had wanted to drink myself to death so many times. And then I told her about Lupe, how I had saved her and how she had, in turn, saved me. It was so liberating to be honest ... just saying how I felt without thinking of how I should have acted or whether what I had done was wrong.

We talked finally about Wendell Pruitt, and I realized that I should probably show the doctor that I had deep remorse, regret and shame for what I had done. But I think Dr. Ortiz was a very smart woman. She would have seen what a lie that was.

We discussed what happened on April 10 ... how my hands were shaking, my heart was racing when Pruitt was choking Lupe. I explained how, when Pruitt stabbed Lupe, I saw a blinding flash of light and different colors, and then everything went black. I told Dr. Ortiz that I didn't remember actually pulling the trigger or seeing Pruitt fall dead on his faded lawn chair and described my next memory as standing at the fence, staring at Pruitt slumped over with blood running down his face. I told Dr. Ortiz that my only thought at the time was to get my dog medical help. The doctor didn't look shocked or appalled. She just nodded solemnly.

After two hours or so, the interview was over and I was physically and mentally drained. But I also felt somehow exhilarated. It was the first time I had ever put my entire life into words. And when I explained it, out loud, I started to feel that perhaps my rotten existence may not have been **all** my fault.

I went home quickly and settled down on the couch for a nap. It had been a long stressful day. Lupe had had her nap while I was gone and was now eager to play. Despite my fatigue, I went to the backyard and we played fetch, a game that involved Lupe bringing back a rope toy and my having to fight with her to get it out of her mouth. She never did understand the objective of "fetch." I called our version, "Toss and Tussle."

After she finally got tired of our game, Lupe went to lie in the yard, on her back with legs wide open as if to soak up as much sun as possible. Given her prior miserable life, I was amazed how Lupe was able to find so many ways to be happy. I sat down on the grass next to her and rubbed her chest and belly. She closed her eyes in quiet contentment.

Maria came outside and we talked. She seemed more relaxed and upbeat than the day before. Apparently, she was going to be meeting David for dinner that evening at El Pinto, a romantic Mexican restaurant in the Alameda neighborhood of north Albuquerque. Maria made sure that I didn't have any objections to her getting together with David and promised me repeatedly that they would not talk about any aspect of my case. I really didn't mind at all. In fact, I was happy for her. She looked very excited.

As we continued to talk, Maria relaxed and shared some of David's personal history with me. I guessed David probably would not have been very happy about these intimate revelations, but I was eager to learn more about my legal advisor and potential "savior."

According to Maria, David was also an only child whose father died from cancer when he was about 13 years old, just two days after his bar mitzvah. David's mother became a depressed, driven and controlling woman who managed her loneliness by living through her son. She demanded that David be the best at everything—music, academics, tennis, the debating team. She crowed about David's accomplishments to her few friends, but admonished him privately for not being better or trying harder.

By the time he went to college in New Mexico, about as far from his mother in New Jersey as he could go, David was understandably afraid of women and unhappy with his life. Maria told me that David relentlessly poked fun at himself, as if he weren't worthy of anyone's attention, and poured his energy and effort into academics. In David's mind, getting A's seemed the only route to achievement and security. Maria, meanwhile, went to college as a brash, hotheaded, angry young woman who dared anyone to challenge or criticize her. But she excelled too.

As fellow outcasts, both insecure and lonely, Maria and David became unlikely fast friends in their freshman year. They talked for hours about politics, movies, ideology and family. David developed a huge crush on Maria, but they graduated before he could work up the nerve to ask her out on a "date." While Maria acknowledged David's longing for her, she denied she had any interest in David romantically during her college years.

Following college, David went straight to law school and Maria left for Seattle. Maria thought that David had chosen to practice law in order to regain some of the power he felt he never had. He was apparently very successful in his legal career, but not in relationships. David had already been through two ugly divorces. He had no children.

Once I learned that David had, in fact, suffered as a child and had to wrestle with his own internal demons, I couldn't help but like him more. We might actually understand each other.

Before I went to sleep that night, I thought of Maria. She had never usually stayed in my thoughts for very long since they had always made me feel sad and guilty. But now I stared at the ceiling, wondering who she was, what kind of life she had led when she left home and if she was glad she had come back to San Sebastian. Maybe Maria was just doing her duty as a daughter. Maybe the last thing she **wanted** to think about was me and my troubles. But, I found, I couldn't stop thinking about her.

Chapter 14

The following week, I accompanied David to some preliminary motions in Sandoval County District Court. It was then that I got to meet the judge who would be presiding over my case, as well as the assistant district attorney who would try to put me in prison.

David had told me on the way to the courthouse that the case had been randomly assigned to a new judge, Bernice Tsosie. He told me that the judge was Navajo, about 40 years old, and only the second Native American woman to sit as a judge in New Mexico. Apparently, Judge Tsosie had been working hard at the New Mexico Attorney General's Office, prosecuting white-collar crimes, when she was tapped for the bench. Since she was so new, she was a blank slate to David.

I was, naturally, very curious about the judge and a few days later, after logging onto the public library's lone computer, I found several feature articles written about her in the Gallup and Farmington newspapers.

According to the features, Bernice Tsosie had been one of seven children and grew up in abject poverty on the Navajo reservation south of Shiprock. Her family had no running water, had to collect wood each day to burn for heat and all seven family members slept together in one room. Apparently, the judge was a very bright girl and excelled in school. She would get up before dawn, do all her chores, walk the three miles each day to the school bus stop and then, after she got home and helped with dinner and fed the animals, she would do her homework by a kerosene lamp after the rest of the family had gone to sleep.

While many of her family told her she was wasting her time with schoolwork, Judge Tsosie was determined to see the world outside the reservation. She became fiercely independent, single-minded and firmly directed, ignoring ridicule from her neighbors and relatives for being "a lost girl" who only wanted to study white men's culture.

Judge Tsosie ended up as a summa cum laude graduate of Princeton University and she received a law degree from Yale. She returned to New Mexico to practice law, to be closer to her roots and also to escape the east coast intellectuals who always singled her out at parties and events as "the smart Indian from out west." Judge Tsosie had never been married and had adopted her late sister's son, who suffered from mental retardation.

I was quite impressed.

The district attorney, on the other hand, was known to all of the trial lawyers and their opinion of her wasn't very reassuring. Monica Morales, a young bright DA with strong political ambitions, would be handling the case for the state. David told me that she was the daughter of the powerful Republican Party leader in the New Mexico Senate. She was very sharp and ambitious, raised in a privileged home and worshipped her father, wanting to follow in his footsteps or perhaps even beyond. Morales had attended Albuquerque's best prep schools, had traveled around the world twice and once dated a prominent movie star who was shooting a film in Santa Fe. While I kept telling myself during the trial that she must have a nice side, I have to admit that I never saw it.

Monica Morales was apparently disliked by almost all the defense attorneys as well as many of her fellow DAs due to her "winner take all" approach to criminal cases. Apparently, she had suffered occasional lapses in judgment and memory when the law required her to disclose important information to the defense.

David told me Morales' nickname amongst the local bar was "The Piranha," and he explained that the word on the street was that she intended to be DA of Sandoval County in a few years, after the present one retired of course. While David was just trying to be open with me, this frightening description of the person who would be prosecuting me sent a cold shiver down my spine.

I had heard of the Morales family, of course. They had made lots of money from multiple auto dealerships in Albuquerque, had aligned themselves with the New Mexico conservatives for some reason and seemed to be on the ballot for everything from Land Commissioner to

Secretary of State. I could see my trial was going to be an important notch on Morales' political belt, perhaps a stepping-stone to higher office. I didn't know David very well yet, but I prayed that he was up to the challenge.

We arrived early to court, and watched as the masses from San Sebastian and other parts of the county filed in to adjudicate their cases. There were men in shackles behind the side bar talking to their attorneys, pregnant women with screaming babies, and the smell of sweat heavy in the air. Everyone but me was dressed in jeans, t-shirts, and sneakers, as if they were just renewing their drivers' licenses. I, on the other hand, had worn my only suit, a threadbare black one that was too big for me now, that I had used only for funerals.

Finally, an officer announced that the court was in session, and a door behind the bench suddenly opened. I then saw a moving crown of black hair heading toward the judge's bench, topping the head of what must be a fairly short person. In the next few seconds, a serious looking woman with caramel brown skin and a round face stood by her tall leather chair, dwarfed by its size. She had short black hair to her shoulders and wire framed half-glasses perched on her nose. The clerk loudly informed all of us that Judge Bernice Tsosie was presiding and, once she was seated, he informed us that we could now sit as well.

I couldn't really hear what was going on in front of the courtroom, but case after case was called, with a lawyer arising from the crowd accompanied by a downcast defendant. Both defendant and attorney would then listen to a bored young prosecutor read the charges to the judge. The lawyers would speak, the judge would speak and shortly another case would be called. An hour passed and suddenly I heard my name, "THE STATE OF NEW MEXICO VERSUS ANASTASIO QUINTANA."

David, who was in front of the court with the other lawyers, motioned me to come forward, and I walked toward him. No one seemed to be paying any attention to me … no one knew yet that I was here for killing a man.

I stood by David and saw the DA get up and approach the bench. She was very attractive, of medium height, quite thin, long dark brown hair streaked with blonde, in a tailored black outfit and very high heels. This was Monica Morales. I guessed by the way she tossed her hair away from her face and by her cocky walk, that she was one of those privileged New

Mexico Latinos who belonged to what we poor folks sometimes call the "Four Hundred Club." The "club" members are the descendants of the original Spanish settlers who had amassed money and property over the centuries and believed they had a ruling interest in the state. They often refer to themselves as being of "Spanish descent" rather than Mexican-American, and feel little connection to the Latinos of other states.

"Monica Morales for the people, your honor," the prosecutor said with authority.

"David Rubin representing Anastasio Quintana, judge."

I stood stock still, my two hands grasping each other in front of me.

Judge Tsosie peered down at us, over the top of her glasses, and softly asked, "OK, What are we here for?"

I could hear that the judge had a slight Navajo accent, which to my ear is English spoken softly, in crisp short syllables, with very little rise and fall of pitch or tone.

Morales raised her chin and, once again, tossed her long hair.

"The Defendant is charged with second degree murder and lesser charges, your honor, in connection with a shooting death that occurred in San Sebastian on April 10 of this year. We are awaiting trial and have some preliminary motions."

Judge Tsosie began to write.

"Go ahead counsel" she said finally.

"First, I would like to move that the defendant's dog, which viciously bit the deceased victim, Wendell Pruitt, be euthanized. The dog is still living with defendant and our community should not be put at any further risk by this dangerous animal."

I audibly gasped and then shouted "NO!"

The courtroom quieted and both the judge and Morales looked at me. I shook my head vigorously, looking pleadingly at the judge and then David.

The judge peered down at me and said, "Mr. Quintana. Hold on. Let's find out what your lawyer has to say."

She then turned to the DA. "And Ms. Morales. I want you to refer to Mr. Quintana by his name from now on. He has not been found guilty of any crime and does not need to be referred to as 'the defendant,' 'the alleged perpetrator' or the like." She hesitated a moment.

"Not in my court anyway."

Morales made a face. David told me later that few judges ever chastised her like this.

"But your honor … "

"You heard me, counselor, right?" the judge interrupted. Morales nodded. "Okay then. Let's hear from Mr. Rubin."

David took a deep breath.

"Your honor, the facts in this case will show that Mr. Pruitt, who has a long and violent criminal record, was trying to kill my client's dog and that he had provoked and grabbed the dog first. By all reports the dog was just trying to defend herself. The dog also suffered from a knife wound from Mr. Pruitt. She is not dangerous by any means. I should add that we also may need the dog as evidence, to show that she is **not** a vicious animal."

David looked at me and smiled slightly.

The judge nodded. "Mr. Quintana can manage the dog, but she never leaves his house without a leash."

Morales started to speak and the judge cut her off.

"Thank you counselors." The judge turned to the DA. "Your motion is denied, Ms. Morales."

Morales, obviously not able to control her facial expressions, pouted and looked at her legal pad. I was surprised she did not stamp her foot.

"Then your honor, I move that the dog be impounded as evidence."

David moved to speak but the judge cut him off.

"No need, counselor." She again looked at Morales with a small smile on her face. "Your motion is DENIED. The dog will remain with Mr. Quintana, leashed at all times she is outside the house."

Morales was silent.

"Anything else?"

"Yes, your honor." Morales glanced again at her legal pad. Reading off several case names, she then looked up and said,

"Based on these precedents, I want to ask that … def … Mr. Quintana….be prohibited from using a 'self-defense' or 'defense of others' approach to his case. There is nothing in the law that allows a person to injure or kill another person in defense of an 'animal'."

Morales said the word "animal" as if it were a deadly spider, crawling up her leg.

David responded quickly by saying that I was entitled to make such a defense as psychiatric and other testimony would show that I WAS acting in self defense, as I identified the dog's life as my own, or something of that nature.

"That is ridiculous, your honor." Morales turned to look at David. "What law do you have to support that?" she barked.

The judge raised her voice.

"Ms. Morales. Do NOT speak to Mr. Rubin directly. You will address all your remarks and arguments to me? Do you understand?"

I could tell that Morales and Judge Tsosie were not off to a good start.

Making another face, the DA turned to the judge. "It doesn't matter what the def … (sigh) … Mr. Quintana was thinking or feeling at the time. How could one rationally confuse themselves with a dog?" The judge put up her palm to Morales.

"So, are you making a temporary insanity defense?" the judge asked David.

"Yes, your honor. I am." Daniel said.

I stood there confused, but not liking what I was hearing. Were they saying I was insane? David had not used this word when he explained our defense to me. What would happen if I was proven crazy? Was it any better to be locked up in a mental hospital than a jail?

David later explained the difference between temporary insanity in criminal trials and a finding that I was unable to make sense of the world due to full-fledged long-term mental illness. Temporary insanity did not require hospitalization or any forcible treatment.

The judge once again glared at Morales.

"Your motion is denied. I will consider whether Mr. Quintana may put on a temporary insanity defense as we get closer to trial, once more evidence has come in. If the evidence meets the minimum threshold for this defense, it will be up to the JURY to decide whether it makes sense to them or is persuasive. YOU can make your arguments during opening and closing at trial."

At this point, Judge Tsosie was not even trying to hide her irritation with Morales.

"Then, your honor, the People request permission to do their own psychiatric evaluation."

"Yes, that is fine," the judge said. "You notify Mr. Rubin of the time and place. But the examiner must be from a list of court-approved psychiatric experts, not someone cherry-picked by the prosecution."

"Now trial dates … " The judge opened a large calendar handed to her by her hovering clerk. After about ten minutes, the two attorneys and the judge were able to schedule two days for trial about eight months later.

"Anything else?" The judge asked. Both attorneys said no.

"Thank you, your honor," Monica Morales said woodenly. She then clicked her pen, tossed her hair and walked away. She had not once looked me in the eye.

The judge watched her go, with an unreadable, but vaguely unfriendly expression. She turned to me and to David and said softly, "Thank you Mr. Rubin. Thank you Mr. Quintana. I will see you in a few months."

As I began to understand later, David planned to show the jury that, at the time I shot Wendell Pruitt, I had been so stressed, panicked and terrified at losing Lupe that I lost control of my reason and the power of choice. My unconscious mind "hijacked" my trigger finger and allowed me to kill Pruitt. Or something like that. This was apparently the definition of temporary insanity and David felt that, with my sad personal history laid out for all to see, and the testimony of Dr. Ortiz, we might be able to show that I was not in control of my actions at the precise time the gun was fired.

Of course, this all rested on the jury's belief that, if I was in my "right mind," I would never have shot another person to protect the life of a dog. I was willing to go along, for Lupe, for Maria and for myself. But I still worried that someone would discover that I actually had no regrets about the death of that horrible man, Wendell Pruitt.

Chapter 15

It was shortly after the pre-trial hearing that the media started to become interested in my case. I don't know who first picked up the story in the regional press, but soon the matter of the **"State of New Mexico vs. Anastasio Quintana"** was on every local radio and television channel and churned around the op-ed pages in the "Albuquerque Journal." Endless debates ensued, with one side calling me a cold-blooded left wing nut who put the life of a dog before that of a fine "American citizen," and the other side appearing pleased that an animal abuser and wife beater had finally gotten his due. Before long, the story had been picked up in newspapers like the "New York Times" and the "Los Angeles Tribune" and as far away as the "BBC" in London. I guess the story of a man shooting and killing another man to protect his dog was just too juicy to pass up.

Requests for interviews started to flood in and I left a message on my telephone answering machine informing callers that all questions should go to David, who thankfully declined every request. I began spotting a few photographers and television reporters peering over my fence and sometimes even boldly knocking at my front door and windows. Whenever they could catch Lupe, Maria or me in the back yard, I saw the cameras flashing.

Most of the news reports weren't as awful as I had expected, seeming to offer some sympathy to the poor, lonely simpleton who loved his dog too much. Of course, Fox Television and Rush Limbaugh's radio broadcast both proclaimed me a poster boy for leftist eco-lunatics. I remember

Limbaugh's annoyingly shrill voice booming, "First illegal immigrants are given the same rights as God-fearing Americans, then enemy combatants, now people protecting their dogs … is this Armageddon?!"

Other television stations invited guests who discussed the value and rights of animals, though only a couple agreed that people should have the right to defend their pets' lives with deadly force (and they were soundly denounced for days afterward). People in the neighborhood looked at me now with a mixture of awe reserved for celebrities and the disgust deserving of a pedophile. Of course, the people of San Sebastian were simple people with uncomplicated lives … they simply didn't know what to make of me or my situation anymore.

David, to his credit, would not speak to the press, though I imagine any lawyer in private practice would have given his eyeteeth for that kind of publicity. David told me that he did not want to prejudice my case by "inflaming passions" any further. He and I had received death threats, but also many unsolicited donations for my defense. I had even being invited to speak at an international animal rights conference! But I did not see myself as a hero, or as a villain. And what I really wanted was to be left alone.

Luckily, the media ruckus didn't last all that long before other news became more pressing. The hottest stories at the time concerned the governor of some Midwest state caught sleeping with his sister-in-law and a series of nail bombs sent to orthodontists on the east coast.

So, life continued on. I was always somewhat anxious and unnerved by the pending trial and the reactions of people around me, but Lupe was my steadying force. We were inseparable. We walked around San Sebastian in the early morning and before the sunset, generally given a wide swath by others. We spent many afternoons in the backyard playing ball or napping together on the couch.

I came to understand that I had never known another person who had offered me a sense of peace and purpose. I had always felt safest being alone, empty and fearful, but free of the impossible expectations and demands of others. I realized I had been incredibly lonely for a very long time. But now, with Lupe, I had a sense of belonging, and the sharp insistent pangs of loneliness and despair had all but disappeared.

Maria and I continued to dance around each other, but I gradually felt more comfortable having her nearby. We didn't express any physical affection and most of our conversations were about chores, the trial, Lupe and what was for dinner. But while I could tell Maria wanted to talk to me and I wanted to talk to her, we remained like two people standing on opposite sides of a river, with no bridge in sight.

Maria began spending quite a lot of time with David. They went out to dinner, on walks along the river, attended a concert at the Sandia Casino, and even went hiking together in the Jemez Mountains. I could tell, based on the way he looked at Maria and the intimate way he would touch her arm, David was falling in love with my daughter. Perhaps he had never fallen out of love with her.

When David talked to me about Maria, he always had a half smile on his face, as if he were a schoolboy caught kissing in the cloakroom. Maria, true to form, kept David at arm's length. She continued to avoid holding hands or kissing, at least when I was around, and always referred to David as "my good friend." Since high school actually, all of Maria's relationships with men ended badly with Maria spurning requests for deeper commitments. She would find even the smallest faults sufficient to cut ties and move on. Perhaps this inability to trust men was my fault too.

I recall the day, perhaps ten years ago, when Maria flew home with a nice man she was dating. Raquel liked him right away—he was Catholic, Mexican-American, had a good job and owned his own home. She liked that he was polite and generous and took care of his elderly parents. Even I liked him, though for some reason I remember also feeling a bit threatened and jealous.

After returning to Seattle, Sam apparently became more and more enamored with Maria. He eventually proposed marriage and told her that he hoped they could live together into old age and have many children and grandchildren together. I remember Maria calling to tell us in a cold stilted tone what should have been wonderful news. I wasn't terribly surprised to hear a week later that she had dumped Sam, claiming that he was too controlling and chauvinistic. Raquel was furious at her. And I, of course, said nothing. Maria never brought anyone to our home again.

While Maria had been a model daughter as a young child, by Raquel's standards anyway, by the time she entered her teens, she had become increasingly headstrong. Maria reveled in putting her shoes on the coffee table, posting racy posters of half-naked boys on her bedroom wall, and writing controversial school papers applauding socialism and decrying militarism. Raquel tried her best to rein Maria in, to get her to be more "ladylike," conservative and quiet, but Raquel eventually gave up, realizing that it always lead to bitter fights.

One Sunday, when Raquel was getting ready to go to Church, Maria decided that she had had enough of the Catholic religion, of ALL religion, and refused to go to Church. Raquel had given up on ME going to Church a long time ago, but the idea that she would now be the only family member to go to Mass pitched her into a fury. She yelled at Maria, threatened her, pleaded with her and eventually tossed out the worst insult she could think of, "Do you want to go to hell with your father?"

I remember the uncomfortable silence that followed, before Maria finally said, "Maybe I do" and quickly left the room. Raquel threw me daggers with her eyes because I just couldn't help smiling at Maria's unusual comment.

As far as I know, Maria never went to Church again. She became a thorn in her mother's side, arguing about everything. She refused to participate in a quinceanera when she turned 15, calling it sexist and silly, and boycotted the senior prom because the school banned a student gay couple who wanted to attend. Yet, she continued to get straight A's in her classes and had many friends.

I could see back then that Maria had been somehow transformed from a polite and meek little girl to a smart woman with a quick temper. She was outspoken and refused to conform to Raquel's, or anyone's, expectations. I couldn't help but admire my daughter for being so strong-willed, but especially marveled at her empathy toward others.

Maria volunteered at the senior citizens center until she was banned for demanding that the nurses be less condescending to the residents. She organized a fundraiser for a homeless and somewhat crazy veteran in the town who everyone else shunned, and even participated in a rally against pedophile priests. Maria's reputation as a radical hothead did not sit well with Raquel, and the mother-daughter relationship that had been so close for so long quickly deteriorated into a series of pitched battles. Maria had become as angry as her mother.

Despite all this, neither Raquel nor Maria paid much attention to me, which was fine. I preferred to be a spectator, with a bottle of beer by my side.

Chapter 16

I got a call one morning in mid-March from David. I remember the New Mexico winter winds were howling outside and the clouds were thick and grey, draped over the peak of the mountain like a slowly moving tidal wave. David reminded me that jury selection was slated to begin on January 20th, joking lamely that with Monica Morales handling the case for the state and Judge Tsosie presiding, the ensuring fireworks would be better suited to July 4th.

After I found out about the start of my trial—a short but terrifying event that would certainly determine my freedom and future—I began to get increasingly depressed and scared. My old instincts, of running away, drinking, sleeping and hiding started to intensify. I spent a lot of time sitting at the kitchen table, staring out the window, sipping coffee and thinking of all the wasted moments of my life. But Lupe would continue to snap me out of it. She would run around in circles, hanging onto a piece of frayed blue rope she had found lying on the sidewalk. She would throw it into the air and then catch it again like a jester trying desperately to cheer up her melancholy king. Lupe would sit with me while I watched television, her head on my thigh, looking at me curiously with her wide brown eyes. Her misshapen ears would angle back and forth, hoping to hear me laugh or say the word "treat" or "walk." Lupe's face was so trusting, so hopeful and so loving that, at odd moments, I would hug her and feel her strength and optimism overpowering my weakness and dread.

Maria had been gone to Seattle for a few weeks, to settle some things there, but she came home the day before the jury selection, calmer and stronger than I had seen her in a long time. She was certain that I would be acquitted, that I would get my life back and that things would be better. Whether she intended to remain a part of my life after the trial was a question I was too afraid to ask.

My daughter seemed at home now, humming as she made meals and vacuumed the rolling balls of dog hair on the floors. She tried to keep intensely busy, but I sometimes found her sleeping on the couch, in the middle of the afternoon, with Lupe nestled besides her. We talked about the trial, she continued to tell me to trust David, and we even chatted about some earlier happy moments of the past, few as they were. But there was still a palpable void between us—A no-man's land of mines and quicksand that could not be navigated without the threat of great harm. And we trod cautiously.

Lupe, as one would expect, had fallen in love with Maria, though she would probably love anyone who was kind to her. She was always delighted to see Maria enter a room. I think Maria was genuinely taken with Lupe's energy, playful nature and persistent need for attention. Maria treated her like a child, with baby talk and expensive dog treats. She even bought Lupe a new red and white candy-striped toy to replace her frayed piece of blue rope (though the rope continued to be her favorite). We became like a family, except with a dog uniting us. To other people this might sound kind of sad or pathetic, but to me, it was a revelation. I never had a family where I actually felt like a member—a member who was wanted and included. With Maria and Lupe as my kin, for once I didn't feel like the outcast or the black sheep. But I knew quite well that ours could be a very short-lived family.

Finally the day of the trial arrived. It was sunny and warm that day, and I put on a new suit that Maria had bought me at a department store. It was dark blue, with thin white stripes, and I thought it was the most beautiful suit I had ever seen. I looked at myself in the mirror and couldn't believe that this skinny old man with gray hair and brown weathered skin, could look like someone important, somebody respectable. There was, perhaps, a gentleman in there somewhere! Maria wore a very nice black dress with a white collar and, while she looked very conservative, she also looked very beautiful.

I remember when Maria was a little girl and her communion was coming up, I took my Friday paycheck and bought her the most expensive communion dress I could afford. It was made of shiny satin fabric and decorated with seed pearls, lace and abalone buttons. It was beautiful. Raquel was furious at the expense, but it was one of the few times I would not relent and absolutely refused to take it back. If Maria couldn't have it, I was going to throw it in the garbage. Or give it to my niece Frieda. That stopped Raquel in her tracks.

I gave the dress to Maria and her expression was magical. Even her mother begrudgingly said, "Que bonita!" to Maria, but then whispered angrily at me, "Hopefully we'll be able to eat next week." At the time, I didn't care if I starved for the next month. I was intoxicated with how beautiful my daughter was and I had told her so. I remember how she smiled at me, a wide and beaming grin, looking at me with more surprise than gratitude. Our connection was soon lost, however, when I got drunk at her communion party and embarrassed her in front of her friends. Today, Maria looked beautiful too, but I couldn't tell her that. I was afraid of what she might remember about the last time I made that comment.

Chapter 17

The trial began right on time, with Judge Tsosie taking the bench at precisely 10 a.m. I sat with David at one long table and the DA sat at the other with her assistant, a fresh-faced but frightened-looking young man with short red hair and freckles covering his nose. In the spectator section were the potential jurors, mostly Latinos who were the predominant population of our county, but also Anglos, Native Americans and even a young African-American woman. I won't bore you with ALL the endless questions that went back and forth between the lawyers, the judge and the potential jurors, but everyone was asked whether they knew or were related to any of the lawyers, the judge or the court personnel. Since so many of the people around San Sebastian are related in one-way or another, or are friendly with family members of the court workers, this eliminated a good dozen people right off the bat.

Questions were asked about how jurors felt about dogs, about whether they had any past convictions, about their political affiliations, any radical or evangelical memberships and the like. Monica Morales strutted around in a tight leather midi dress, trying to intimidate jurors she thought would be sympathetic to me—like elderly Latino women, poor people and dog owners. She would then try to have these folks dismissed "for cause," which I learned later meant they were inherently prejudiced in my favor. Judge Tsotsie dismissed most of Morales' requests as improper grounds for exclusion. Again and again, Morales tried to refer to me as the defendant, the assailant and even once as the killer of an innocent man, but the judge interrupted her each time and insisted she call me by my name.

David had explained to me on prior occasions that he would try to impanel jurors who were educated and, thus, not intimidated by the prosecution—jurors who were creative free-thinkers like writers and artists, and people who were not overtly religious, conservative or patriotic, like military families. Hardcore bikers were out too, though I don't think there were any in the jury pool. David probed their occupations, religious attendance, levels of education, views of mental illness and perspectives on the role of law in society.

At the end of four exhausting hours, both sides had agreed to impanel an odd group of 14 people, twelve jurors and two alternates. There were eight women and six men. Seven of the 14 were over 50 years old and nine jurors had never attended college. There were nine New Mexican Latinos, a member of the San Felipe Indian tribe and four middle- aged Anglos, a man and three women. After jury selection was completed, the judge instructed everyone to be back the following morning. We were released, and I went home to fret again about my fate.

When we got home, Lupe was waiting for me at the front window, as usual, and it lightened my heart. Not even a trial to determine whether I was to spend my life behind bars could keep her from seeing me as anything but her trusted friend.

Maria and I talked a bit about the jurors and she seemed to feel as though they were a decent lot. The people she most disliked—the stuffy engineer, the overly made-up real estate agent and the self-righteous minister, had been excused. I know she thought the world of David and completely believed he would win an acquittal. But I had never had much luck in the past and was somewhat doubtful that my fortunes would change now.

Pessimistically, I kept thinking how much I would miss Lupe and our walks under the cottonwood trees.

David took Maria out to dinner the next night and I was happy to be able to have an evening when I didn't have to talk about or ponder the mysteries of the upcoming trial. I was happy to see Maria so excited getting ready for her evening out. She and I had continued to become less awkward around each other, but we still could only get so close before something pushed us apart again. Maria did not talk much about her childhood or memories she had when she was young. We did not talk about Raquel, except in passing, nor did Maria reveal much about her life back in Seattle. We slid around the meaty issues, talking as always about the weather, Mexican food, San Sebastian gossip and, of course, the ever-present force of nature—Lupe.

As I sat that evening with Lupe, watching a foolish made-for-television movie about werewolves, I tried to allow myself the pleasure of enjoying the moment, the quiet time Lupe and I had to relax together. No expectations, no disappointments, just easy contentment. Given my potential future in a prison cell, I wanted to enjoy every second of this peace, and of the true friendship that I had so missed in my life. But the trial hung over me like a huge broken tree limb.

By the time Maria came home that night, Lupe and I had gone to sleep. I remember dreaming about the beach that night, somewhere with palm trees, a feeling of warmth and calm. Suddenly the beach became an island and I saw Maria and Lupe on a small boat, sailing off into the sunset ... without me. I tried to scream, but I had no voice. I tried to jump in the water and swim, but my legs wouldn't move. The boat sailed further and further out of sight until it was gone and, just then, I found myself in complete darkness.

Chapter 18

The trial began on a typical San Sebastian day; a clear blue sky with thin white clouds slowly floating overhead. I was shaking when I put on my suit, and asked Maria to help me with my tie. She smiled when she did it but had much sadness in her eyes. Despite her frequent and loudly proclaimed optimism, I could tell she was scared as well.

I have learned from my many hours watching dog-training experts on television, that canines have an amazing ability to sense when something is wrong. I noticed that Lupe was somewhat subdued that morning. She lay in a corner of the bedroom watching me warily and then later sat quietly under the kitchen table, not even begging for a piece of bacon or scrap of toast. Lupe didn't know why I was so scared or what awaited me. But she could tell that this day was different from most others. Just before we left the house, Lupe quietly went to lie on my bed and put her head down on my pillow, staring at me sadly. I petted her head and told her we would take a long walk later.

When we arrived at the courthouse, there were at least a dozen television cameras and a clot of reporters who converged on Maria and me as we walked up the front steps. I saw microphone tags of CNN and Fox TV. Even the BBC was back. I remember wondering how my pathetic story could be of interest to anyone halfway around the world?

Then the microphones were shoved in my face, one of them hitting me hard on the chin. "Mr. Quintana, would you kill again to save your dog?"

"Hey, Anastasio, do you have anything to say to Wendell Pruitt's family?"

"Uh, Quintana, you there, do you think it's okay to kill people to save animals? Do you think you did the right thing?"

"Are you afraid of going to prison? Is this your daughter? Lady, is this your father?"

My head was spinning. I had never had so many people focused on me and yelling at me at the same time. I had always gone virtually unnoticed in a crowd. Now, my mouth hung open and my legs froze in place. Luckily, Maria grabbed me by the elbow and marched me up the steps and through the front door, putting her finger up to her lips when she glanced at me and pushing forcefully through the group of reporters with an outstretched palm.

David was waiting and came over to us. He gently touched Maria on the hand. I saw something in his eyes that told me this was more than a cordial greeting, but Maria just smiled uncomfortably and politely moved her arm away.

When David turned to me, he grabbed my shoulder with a strong hand and told me that we should go up to the courtroom and sit down. I soon saw the DA across the large front entryway talking excitedly to several other attorneys. She glanced for just a moment in my direction before turning on her high heels and walking briskly down the hall.

Maria sniffed when she saw Morales.

"The bitch is wearing **red** … what does she think this is, the senior prom?" I was happy to have Maria on MY side.

We entered the courtroom doors and, as I looked around the room, I saw there were rows of spectators already waiting. David told me to look straight ahead and pay no attention to who was observing. I still caught a glimpse of a fat biker with a leather vest and tattoos, sitting near the aisle, arms crossed and frowning at me as I walked by.

After I sat down, I rubbed my face with both hands. I remember feeling confused and terrified and resigned at the same time. I couldn't change what I had done, so I would have to accept the consequences. But why did I have to be paraded out in public like this—like … an accused Salem witch?

David had already explained to me what would happen each step of the trial, but I couldn't seem to recall anything he had told me. I rested my folded hands on the table, trying not to think of anything but Lupe waiting for me back home. My heart was beating rapidly and I was sweating in my new wool suit.

Finally, after the DA came strutting in, her assistant carrying her briefcase and a dozen large folding files, the bailiff announced the judge. The door swung open and a black-robed Judge Tsosie calmly and quietly sat down at the bench and nodded at David and me and then at the DA.

The court bailiff bellowed. "THIS COURT IS NOW IN SESSION. THE HONORABLE JUDGE BERNICE TSOSIE PRESIDING. YOU MAY SIT DOWN."

There were several minutes of silence as Judge Tsosie wrote something.

She turned to the clerk.

"You may now call the case," she said quietly

"Now hearing The State of New Mexico versus Anastasio Luis Quintana"

The judge cleared her throat, then looked to the jury.

"Ladies and Gentleman of the jury, we are here today to decide the case of the State of New Mexico versus Mr. Anastasio Quintana. I ask that you listen carefully and quietly, and you may write down notes to yourself that you cannot share with anyone else, not even the other jurors. If you need to ask a question, you may write it down and pass it to the court bailiff, Mr. Archuleta, who will bring it to my attention. You have taken an oath to fairly and fully consider the evidence presented and to render a decision consistent with your understanding of the facts and the law. There should be no room for passion or prejudice, but only a willingness to make a fair decision, based on the standard 'beyond a reasonable doubt.' Of course, I will give you detailed instructions at the end of the evidentiary portion of the trial. Okay? Any questions?"

The jury looked at the judge silently and solemnly.

"Good. Then let's proceed. Ms. Morales, you may give your opening."

Monica Morales stood up, smoothed out her scarlet dress and then went to a podium at the front of the courtroom, facing the jury. She looked a bit nervous, but also wore what seemed to be a practiced angry expression. She fiercely tossed her hair over her shoulder like a wrestler ready for her first grapple.

"Ladies and gentlemen of the jury. We are here today to decide whether Mr. Anastasio Quintana is guilty of the killing of another human being without just cause. The facts will show you, very clearly, that Mr. Quintana, in defense of his dog … his DOG … shot and killed his next-door neighbor, Wendell Pruitt, who was not threatening Mr. Quintana with bodily harm in any way. In fact, this good man was simply sitting in his own yard, divided from Mr. Quintana's yard by a five foot picket fence, when the defendant … um …"

Morales glanced at the judge whose eyes had narrowed a bit.

" … excuse me … when Mr. Quintana left the argument, went into his house, took his gun, and returned to Mr. Pruitt. He then aimed the gun at his neighbor, and shot him squarely in the forehead."

Morales referred to her notes for a moment.

"The coroner will tell you that Mr. Pruitt died instantly. Mr. Quintana's attorney will no doubt suggest that his client was defending his dog's life from Mr. Pruitt. While there is no convincing evidence that Mr. Pruitt meant the dog any harm, even if he DID try to hurt or even kill the dog, the laws of New Mexico simply do not allow a human being to kill another human being, except in defense of himself or ANOTHER HUMAN BEING."

Morales was starting to sound louder and more confident, and began to strut alongside the jury box. The judge quickly instructed Morales to remain at the podium.

"We will also present evidence that Mr. Quintana was a violent man, a habitual alcoholic, with a grudge against Mr. Pruitt, who very likely used his dog as an excuse to kill his neighbor. Facts will show that these men had had a troubled relationship prior to this incident, bad enough for Mr. Quintana to wish Mr. Pruitt harm."

Morales hesitated and pointed her index finger upward.

"HOWEVER, even if Mr. Quintana DID murder Mr. Pruitt over genuine love of his DOG, or whatever supposed harm the deceased threatened to the dog, you still must find Mr. Quintana GUILTY. That is the law. That is what you have sworn to follow. Thank you."

With that, Morales grabbed her notes and took her seat at the DA's table, a small satisfied grin on her face. Apparently, this was becoming the dream case for a young prosecutor, as it was getting a boatload of publicity. David had told me that Morales called a press conference the day before and had posed for the cameras like a movie star on the red carpet.

The judge looked at David.

"Mr. Rubin?"

"Thank you, your honor." David patted me on the shoulder, glanced at Maria in the front spectator row and sighed as he got to the podium.

"Ladies and gentleman of the jury. My name is David Rubin and I am honored to represent Anastasio Quintana. Mr. Quintana was born and raised in San Sebastian, brought up a family here, worked diligently as a plumber in the community for decades and has never been convicted of anything in his life. He has been a law-abiding man and has never provoked a fight with anyone."

David leaned toward the jury, lowering his head for a moment.

"Mr. Quintana is also a simple man who minds his own business, doesn't bother other people, and has happily lived alone in his simple house with his dog Lupe, who he rescued after she was left injured and bleeding at the side of the road. What happened to Mr. Pruitt was, of course, a tragedy. However, the evidence will show you that Mr. Pruitt instigated this horrible incident by kidnapping my client's dog, putting a knife to her throat, actually stabbing her in the throat, and threatening to kill her in front of my client. All because she was barking. Yes, a fence separated them and nothing my client could say would dissuade Mr. Pruitt from threatening the dog with death. This highly aggressive and hostile behavior led my client to panic, a degree of panic that resulted in his being unable to control what he did next."

David hesitated for a minute as he caught his breath. Maria had told me that David was prone to nervous rapid-fire speech, having a tendency to talk louder and faster with each passing minute. This, of course, did not work well in New Mexico, where folks generally converse calmly and slowly. When David began speaking again, it was unrushed and deliberate.

"We will present psychiatric testimony that, at the time of the shooting, Mr. Quintana did not have control over his actions, did not even remember what he did until much later. In essence, my client had a period of "dissociation" or "depersonalization.""

David pronounced these two words very slowly and distinctly, perhaps to make an impression with the jury about how important they were to be in this trial.

"Dissociation and Depersonalization." David repeated. "That's what psychiatrists call it. In terms that are more familiar to the general public, my client suffered from 'temporary insanity,' as he was unable to control his actions or appreciate their wrongfulness.

David cleared his throat and studied the jury for a moment.

"Now, I know that you probably wonder if it is even possible to be temporarily insane. The prosecution will certainly ridicule the idea. But after listening to the testimony, you will conclude that Mr. Quintana led a difficult and sometimes tragic life, with many emotional challenges. You will see that he was, IS, utterly devoted, and perhaps obsessed with his dog. She means everything to him. This horrific episode with Wendell Pruitt, where Mr. Quintana was faced with losing his companion, triggered a reaction that caused him to lose control of his reasoning ability and his self-control. As a result, he did not knowingly kill Wendell Pruitt. We will present an expert witness, an eminent and respected psychiatrist, who can explain this to you so that you will clearly understand that my client did not know what he was doing at the time the fatal shot was fired. These **unconscious** actions were the ones that resulted in Wendell Pruitt's death."

David looked seriously at the jurors for a moment.

"After you hear all the evidence, you will understand what happened the day of the argument and you will find my client NOT GUILTY. Thank you."

David walked slowly back to our table, a sad look on his face. I glanced at the jury and they were all looking at me, probably searching for signs of insanity or dementia. The DA, however, was turned around, chuckling with an assistant who sat in back of her. She must have really believed my case was a "slam dunk," an easy murder conviction for another important notch on her belt.

Morales was still talking when the judge interrupted her.

"Excuse me. Are you ready to call your first witness, Ms. Morales?" the judge asked sternly.

Morales quickly turned around and wiped the smile off of her face.

"Oh. Yes, your honor. I call San Sebastian police officer Benny Chavez."

My neighbor Benny got up from somewhere in back of me and warily approached the witness stand. Judge Tsosie swore him in and he sat down, finally looking briefly in my direction. He then turned away.

Morales came and stood in front of Benny.

"Officer Chavez, do you recall the night of April 10?"

"Yes. I do." Benny's voice was hoarse, and he cleared his throat.

"What happened about 9 p.m. that day?"

"I was dispatched to 206 Maldonado Road in San Sebastian due to a neighbor hearing a gunshot there."

"What did you find?"

"I found a Mr. Wendell Pruitt in his back yard, sitting in a lawn chair, dead from a single gunshot wound to his head."

"What else did you learn?"

Benny looked at her for a moment.

"I didn't learn anything else. What do you mean?"

Morales looked down in frustration.

"Okay, what happened next, then?"

"Oh. I called for backup immediately and the station sent someone from forensics. Officer Clement. She determined that the shot had most likely come from the direction of the deceased's neighbor, at ... 220 Tenorio Lane. We later determined that to be the home of Mr. Anastasio Quintana."

"Is that Mr. Quintana sitting there?" She pointed her red fingernail in my direction.

Benny scrunched his brow.

"Well yes, of course." He was obviously not used to the evidentiary rhythm of a murder trial.

"Was Mr. Quintana home at the time you went to his house to investigate?"

"No."

"When did you next see Mr. Quintana?"

"It was about an hour later, he came back to his house with his dog. The dog was all bandaged ... "

Morales made a face and cut him off abruptly.

"Officer, please do not add information. Just answer the questions I asked you."

"Fine." Benny crossed his arms defensively.

I can tell you from personal experience that people in San Sebastian do not like to be chastised or scolded in public. It's considered rude and threatening—the kind of thing you'd expect in Chicago, New York or even Albuquerque. In our town, Morales should have smiled and asked the officer to try not to make that mistake again. I imagined Benny was starting to feel threatened and angry.

"Now, after you and the other officer spoke to Mr. Quintana, what, if anything did you discover?"

"Mr. Quintana seemed confused, very dazed and … "

Morales raised her voice.

"I did not ask you how Mr. Quintana SEEMED … please, listen to my question, officer!"

She glared at him.

"Now, again, what did you discover about WHO murdered Mr. Pruitt?"
"OBJECTION." Daniel was suddenly on his feet.

"Your objection, counsel? The judge peered over her glasses.

"No one has yet established that Mr. Pruitt was MURDERED, or what had happened. The DA should not put words into the witness's mouth."

"Sustained." The judge looked at Morales, daring her to argue further.

Morales looked peeved. She sighed and looked again at the officer.

"Officer Chavez, what did Mr. Quintana tell you after he arrived back at his house?"

"Okay. I asked him what happened. He just looked at me kind of confused. I told him that his neighbor across the fence was shot to death. We asked him if he knew who might have shot him, and he said, 'I must have.' We found a recently fired gun lying in the grass in his backyard."

"Was this the gun used to kill Mr. Pruitt?"

"Ballistics said it was."

"Did you ask Mr. Quintana why he thought he had killed the victim?"

"Yes. He thought for a moment and said … " Benny hesitated.

"Yes, officer … "

"He said, 'the bastard was trying to kill my dog.' "

"Thank you, officer.

Morales turned halfway to leave and then turned back to him.

"Oh, by the way, Officer Chavez, did Mr. Pruitt have any other injuries other than the head wound?"

"Yes, ma'am. He had a couple of puncture wounds on his left hand."

"A recent injury?"

"It looked fairly fresh at the time."

"A dog bite, perhaps?"

"Maybe."

"Thank you." Morales stomped to her table.

Benny watched her for a moment. Suddenly he said loudly, "It was really just a scratch."

Morales turned suddenly, glared in Benny's direction and said "That's ALL, officer! I have no more questions, your honor."

Benny shrugged.

David cleared his throat and approached the officer.

"So, Officer, I heard you testify that, after you asked Mr. Quintana who killed Mr. Pruitt, my client said "I MUST HAVE."

"Yes."

"Did you think that was peculiar?"

"Yes. I asked him what he meant."

"And what did he respond … ?"

"He said he couldn't remember raising the gun or pulling the trigger, or Mr. Pruitt even being shot. He said the next thing he remembered, after pointing the gun at the deceased, was seeing him slumped over in a chair, with blood on his head."

"What did he do after he saw Mr. Pruitt dead in the lawn chair."

"He took his dog and drove off."

"Did he tell you where was he going?"

"He told me that he took his dog to the doctor … the veterinarian, I mean."

"Why was that?"

"He said Mr. Pruitt had tried to kill her and he needed to save her life."

David moved closer to Benny.

"Now, Officer Chavez, prior to the night of the incident, were you familiar with the deceased, Wendell Pruitt?"

Morales saw what was coming and rose quickly.

"OBJECTION!"

Without waiting for the judge to inquire about her objection, she asked rather indignantly, "May we approach?"

"Yes, counsel. Approach." The judge leaned forward.

David later told me that Morales cited the rules of evidence that state one cannot besmirch the reputation of the deceased to inflame the prejudices of the jury, that Pruitt was not on trial and that David should not be allowed to ask questions about his past involvement with neighbors or the police … what is called "character evidence."

David said he reminded the judge that during the opening statement, Morales briefly described Mr. Pruitt as a "good man" who was just sitting in his yard, minding his own business. This description of him as "a good man" therefore opened the door for questions about his reputation. In other words, if I could be accused of killing a "good" man, I should have the opportunity to show that he really wasn't so good.

The judge nodded. The lawyers stepped away from the bench.

"Objection is overruled. Ms. Morales, you opened the door, now Mr. Rubin can walk through it."

Morales opened her mouth to object further, but the judge held up her hand and looked at Morales with a stony face. Morales closed her mouth into a pout. The judge leaned towards her.

"OVERRULED, Ms. Morales. I don't plan to argue with you about my rulings."

David smiled again at Benny.

"Now, Officer Chavez, Where were we?"

David was obviously enjoying his minor victory.

"Ah yes, I asked you if Mr. Pruitt was known to your department prior to the night of the incident."

"Oh, yes."

"In what way?"

"Well, we had been to the house probably dozens of times over the last two years. Pruitt was part of a "bad" biker gang … "

Morales objected. "Where is the proof that the deceased was part of a gang? This is speculation."

The judge said calmly, "Mr. Rubin, will the witness be able to verify that Mr. Pruitt was part of an organized gang?"

"Yes, I believe so, your honor."

"Then I will allow you to ask that question first. Objection overruled."

Morales was starting to look flustered and did not flip back her hair before sitting down this time. A think lock hung limply in front of her right eye.

"Ok, officer. How do you know that Mr. Pruitt was in a gang?"

"Well, we know there is a gang called the Rebellious Monsters from Hell or RMFH. Mr. Pruitt had the tattoos that signify his membership, he wears the emblem on his jacket and … he told me."

"Told you what?"

"That he was a gang member of the Rebellious Monsters from Hell."

"When did he tell you that?"

"Every time we went to his house. I think he thought it sounded intimidating."

"OBJECTION!" Morales yelled. "Officer Chavez couldn't read Mr. Pruitt's mind to determine how he *wanted* to sound."

This time the judge sustained the objection.

David continued unflustered. "Now, what resulted in the dozens of visits to Mr. Pruitt over the past two years?"

"Mostly complaints from the neighbors about noise, about drinking, about beer bottles being thrown at cars. Um … fights, domestic abuse, even a knife being drawn on someone. And drugs. Cocaine, pot, ecstasy, heroin once …"

"Was Mr. Pruitt ever arrested?"

"Yes, probably about five times, for disturbing the peace, assault, vagrancy, possession, indecent exposure … We never were able to show he was dealing …"

"OBJECTION!" Morales said without her usual vigor.

The judge quickly sustained the objection. Morales' second tiny victory permitted her a subtle Mona Lisa grin.

The judge turned to the jury. "The jury will disregard the officer's last comment."

David continued. "Did any of Mr. Pruitt's close neighbors complain to the police?"

"Yes. And Mr. Quintana's late wife, Raquel, called frequently."

"Did Mr. Pruitt ever mention her by name?"

"Yes, I … he did."

"What did he say?"

Benny immediately looked uncomfortable and rubbed his palm across his forehead.

"Okay … this is hard to do here … he called her a … " Benny hesitated again.

"Go ahead, it's alright," David said.

"He called her a "Stupid Spic Bitch.""

I glanced at the jury. They frowned, looking disturbed. Morales, alarmed, rose to object but then sat down again without speaking a word.

"Did you consider Mr. Pruitt to have been a violent man?"

"OBJECTION!!!" Morales was up on her feet again.

"Sustained." The judge looked at Daniel.

"Foundation, counsel."

"Yes, thank you your honor. Officer Chavez, did you have any cause to witness Mr. Pruitt being physically assaultive toward other people?":

"Yes. On one visit, we found him waving one of the kitchen knives at his girlfriend, who was backed into a corner. Another time, he had gotten into a fight with another … houseguest you could call him … and the guy had a broken nose. Mr. Pruitt's fist was covered in blood. He admitted he beat up the guy really bad for smiling at his lady. The victim didn't want to press charges."

"Thank you. No further questions for this witness."

David took his seat and I looked down at the table, suddenly feeling very sad about Raquel, about what she had gone through with Pruitt. That I had done nothing to defend her …

The judge looked at the clock on the wall and then said, "Do we have time for another witness before the lunch break?"

Morales rose and said yes. She called the forensic expert, Darlene Clement, to the stand. The witness was a tough-looking woman, middle aged, with a short square haircut. She was somewhat overweight and packed tightly into her police uniform. She looked almost nonchalant about her day in court and did not even glance at the defense table.

After the preliminary qualifications were settled, Officer Clement was deemed an expert. She testified that the angle of the gun, the trajectory of the bullet, the extent of the injuries indicated that the bullet that killed Wendell Pruitt came from a .38 caliber handgun from about fifteen feet away at slightly downward angle. When asked about the direction the bullet had come from, she concluded that it had come from the southwestern edge of my yard.

Morales paced back and forth.

"Did you compare the bullet found in the deceased's body to the gun found in Mr. Quintana's yard?"

"Yes. The bullet was from that gun. It had the same barrel striations."

"Who was the gun registered to?"

"Anastasio Quintana." Clement then looked at me for the first time and pointed her finger. "Him. He was the perp."

David half rose to object, but then realized there would be no purpose to it. I was the one who shot and killed Wendell Pruitt, after all.

David did not have many questions for the witness. Essentially, he had her state that she knew nothing of the circumstances surrounding the shooting, and that the forensic evidence could not show motive.

We broke for lunch and David, Maria and I went into one of the empty side rooms to eat. Maria looked tired and frightened, and as she sat down, she looked at me woefully. She had moved out of our house well before Pruitt had moved into the neighborhood and had no inkling about how miserable he had made our lives.

I quickly got up and went into the adjacent bathroom to collect my thoughts. I washed my face and looked in the mirror ... trying to see what Morales saw—the face of a murderer, of a man who could cavalierly kill another man with a single clean shot to the forehead and then go take his dog to the veterinarian. I didn't see a cold-blooded murderer's face.

I then looked for the eyes that had greeted me in the mirror most of my life … empty and sad with no spark of life or hope. But my eyes were not hard, cold or lifeless. They looked frightened and tired, but also had clarity. A spark of something. I think I finally *wanted* to have a future.

When I came out of the bathroom, I noticed that Maria and David were holding hands and talking with their heads very close together. I could see David was consoling Maria, but not many lawyers would ordinarily expect a client's daughter to put her hand gently on his cheek. I backed up, cleared my throat and then reentered the room to eat my sandwich. Maria and David quickly moved apart.

I was strangely famished, as if this would be the last meal of my life. I was also exhausted and wished I were back at home, sitting on the porch, listening to my music with Lupe stretched out nearby.

Chapter 19

The afternoon session began precisely at 2 o'clock. The judge and jury entered, and things got rolling quickly. Morales called her next witness, a short stocky elderly woman, with dyed black hair piled high on her round head. She entered the courtroom with a cocky stride, despite her cane, and wore flamboyantly applied makeup. She carried a pocketbook that looked bigger than David's briefcase. I recognized her immediately. It was my sister-in- law Cora Espinosa, Raquel's oldest sister. I heard Maria gasp in back of me.

Cora sat down in the witness seat and looked at me with a nasty smirk. We had never liked each other, and I knew she blamed me for Raquel's unhappiness and frustrations. In later years, even Raquel got tired of Cora's lectures about how to live her life and told her sister to go to hell. The two had not spoken for years before Raquel's death, and Cora hadn't even attended her younger sister's funeral.

David had already told me that Cora was one of the many people on the prosecutor's witness list as a potential "character" witness. Given her lousy character, I couldn't imagine her passing judgment on mine.

David and I had talked about my relationship with Cora, and what she would probably say about me. I didn't mention her possible testimony to Maria because I knew she would feel betrayed and furious and probably try to confront her aunt. I really didn't want Maria to listen to Cora's lies about me, or about the horrible truths either. David, of course, could not tell Maria about Cora's possible appearance at trial without my permission and, on this rare occasion, I denied it.

David asked to approach the bench. He apparently told the judge that the witness was there to malign my character and to tell irrelevant stories about my past behavior and my drinking problems. He argued that it was more prejudicial than probative, which, I learned later, means that the bad impressions of me that it would create with the jury would outweigh and overshadow the truth about what happened to Wendell Pruitt.

Morales, however, was ready. She argued that because my defense was that I was a simple person, with no criminal record, minding my own business, who shot someone while being temporarily insane, she had the right to try to establish a motive—that I was a lout, a drunk, I owned a gun, I was sometimes irrational and full of rage and had reason to kill a man who made my family's life hell and called my wife a "a stupid spic bitch."

As David expected, the judge overruled his objection. But she sternly warned Morales to stay within the rigid boundaries of motive for this crime. She said she would not allow a general character assassination as a way of getting a conviction.

Morales smiled warmly as she approached Cora, who was actually fanning herself with a bright gold "abenica," a souvenir she once bought while visiting Spain. Cora was always putting on airs, despite having been born in an unheated one-room shack in Cloudcroft, New Mexico.

"Mrs. Espinosa, what is your relationship with the defendant … or rather, Mr. Quintana? Sorry, your honor."

"He was the husband of my late sister, may she rest in peace, sweet Jesus" Cora crossed herself for dramatic effect.

"Mr. Quintana's wife, was she your younger sister?"

"Yes. By about eight years."

I knew it was more like fourteen. Raquel often complained that, with Cora, she got two overbearing, demanding mothers, both who favored straps over lectures.

"When did you first meet Mr. Quintana?"

"Oh, I knew him since he was born. The Quintanas lived in an old ugly house over on San Felipe Ave. He went to school with my sister and we saw him at Church, the few times he decided to go." She again glared at me.

"OBJECTION!"

"Sustained." The judge looked sternly at Cora. "No more inserting your opinions, Mrs. Espinosa. Listen to what Ms. Morales asks you."

Cora squinted briefly at the judge and then turned around without responding. I knew how she felt about Native Americans, always telling people they were dirty, stupid and had "diseases." I'm sure she was dying to let slip a nasty and bigoted remark, and I sort of hoped she would so jurors could see the real Cora.

"How old were your sister and Mr. Quintana when they got married?"

"About 19, 20 maybe. I told her not to marry him. He and his family were no good."

The judge cleared her throat ominously.

Morales got it. She nodded at the judge.

"Now, Mrs. Espinosa. We are talking here about Mr. Quintana. We do not need to hear anything about the rest of his family, okay?"

"Sure." Cora kept fanning her sunken, garishly painted cheeks.

"Now, did your sister voice to you any problems she had with Mr. Quintana during the marriage regarding drinking … "

"Yes, he was an awful drunk. He drank constantly. I don't know when he was ever sober. And a MEAN drunk too. I just told my sister to take her daughter Maria and leave. I worried about her safety. Who knows what he was going to do one day!?"

Cora smirked, thinking she was very clever …

David whispered in my ear that he had plenty of grounds to object to most of what Cora was saying, but that he thought it was better to let her talk and then hang her in the cross examination.. I nodded. I just wished I could be allowed to leave the courtroom while she was up there. Or at least to throw something at her.

"Do you remember any incidents when he was violent?"

"Yes. I remember when he threw my sister against the wall after she refused to make him fresh tortillas, following a drunken bender one night. She had bruises on her shoulder, a bump on her head and a twisted ankle, I think."

I whispered to David that that was actually what Cora's husband did to her after she threw a pan of tortillas at his face one night. He glanced back and whispered, "I know."

"Did you hear anything from either your sister or Mr. Quintana about their neighbor, Mr. Pruitt?"

"Who?"

"Wendell Pruitt." The man who moved into the house in back of your sister's house."

"Like what?"

Morales sighed, frustrated. "Like them having any problem with him. With noise or other … things?"

"I think she did." Cora thought a moment. "Oh, yes. They were the drunks that hung out with Anastasio, I think."

"Um … "

Morales quickly wrapped up, knowing that she had a loose cannon on her hands. The prosecutor had probably prepped Cora to testify in a certain way, but Cora always did and said what she wanted.

"Do you think your brother-in-law was an angry person?"

"Yes."

"Do you think he was capable of murdering someone … "

OBJECTION! Daniel shouted before Cora could open her fat mouth.

"Withdrawn. I'm done, your honor." Morales pranced back to her seat, one again confidently flipping back her hair before she sat down.

David wrote on a pad, "This should be good … "

He then rose to cross-examine the decrepit old liar on the stand. As he approached, Cora dramatically folded her fan with a click and refused to look David in the eyes. She had the same look as when she didn't get her way in the family. She would grimace, cross her arms and storm out. Of course, she couldn't storm out now …

"Mrs. Espinosa?" David started.

"Yes."

"Now, my records indicate that you are fourteen years older than your sister Raquel was, not eight. Is that correct?"

She frowned. "I don't know. I can't remember."

"Well, you have five siblings in between you and your sister Raquel, no multiple births. How could it be four years?"

"It was." Her voice was weak. The jury looked at her with surprise.

"Here is a family photo when your sister was only a baby. Is that you standing next to your father, a young teenager?" She looked at the photo, blushed and quietly said. "I don't know. No. Yes. I'm an old lady, I can't remember everything."

"But you remember everything about your brother-in-law, don't you?"

"OBJECTION!"

"Withdrawn."

David paused. He had already established Cora as a practiced liar in front of the jury. I suppressed a smile.

I heard Maria whisper behind me, "That fuckin' old bitch"

Daniel continued. "You said that Mr. Quintana was violent, is that right?"

"Yes, that's what I said. Don't you listen?" Cora didn't much like Jews either and she glared at David with disgust.

"Alright, then. I have an old Sandoval County criminal court record here that says that, in 1986, you swore out a complaint in court that your husband came home drunk one night and pushed you against the wall when you threw a plate of tortillas at him. Isn't that right?"

"No, that happened to my sister."

Daniel waved the document. "But, it is right here. You also had the same injuries you said your sister had, a bruise on the shoulder, a bump on the head and a twisted ankle. Do you want to read this to refresh your memory?"

"NO!"

"Are you telling the jury then, that the very same incident, involving a pan of tortillas and causing the very same injuries, happened to both you AND your sister?"

Cora slunk back in her chair, as if she had been caught stealing pencils at school.

"Why not? My husband was no angel."

David smiled at the jury.

"Now, Mr. Quintana admits to having had a drinking problem. As far as you know, did he ever stop supporting his family financially?"

"I don't know."

David held up some papers. "This set of documents here is Mr. Quintana's work history." David brought it closer to Cora's face. She scowled and looked away.

"He was only absent from work eight days in 30 years at his job. Does that sound like someone who couldn't earn a living or support his family?"

Cora leaned forward, wiping away a drop of sweat running down the side of her head.

"Stop asking me these questions."

The judge peered down to Cora.

"Just answer the questions put to you, ma'am."

Cora looked back at the judge with disdain, squinted menacingly and started to speak. However, she then closed her mouth and turned away. Finally, she yelled,

"I DON'T KNOW!"

"And, Ms. Espinosa, you say you were close to your sister, right?"

"Yes, we were very close."

"Oh. Could you tell me why you didn't attend your sister's funeral?"

Cora turned bright red and started fanning herself like crazy.

"I may have been sick … "

"Isn't it true that your own sister told you to stay out of her life, to keep away from her home and family?"

"OBJECTION! Hearsay." Morales was on her feet.

The judge frowned at her. "Ms. Morales, do I need to tell you that hearsay applies to living persons who have the opportunity to be present and offer their own testimony. Obviously, Raquel Quintana is not able to do so. AND this is for impeachment purposes."

Morales sat down silently. She turned red.

"Objection overruled."

"Well? … " David persisted. He moved closer to Cora.

"What?!" Cora pulled out her fan again, using it as a wedge between David and her.

"Isn't it true that, for the last eight years of her life, you did not speak one word to your younger sister Raquel?"

Cora started to cry.

"He turned her against me." She pointed her finger at me with a snarl on her face that would scare the devil. "He is a murderer!"

"No further questions, your honor." David sat down.

"Any redirect?"

Morales looked dejected.

"Nothing, your honor."

"The witness is excused."

Without looking at anyone in the courtroom, Cora grabbed her cane and gargantuan pocketbook and hobbled quickly from the courtroom. I looked at David with renewed respect. He had taken down the family's old nightmare with only a few questions.

"Next witness?"

Morales stood up and announced, "We call Dr. George Ogilvy."

Dr. Ogilvy was the prosecution's "expert" psychologist, who had spent an hour or two, a few months earlier, asking me to perform silly tasks like unscrambling words, interpreting proverbs and counting backwards by sevens. I remember being very scared at the time, thinking this "expert" was going to pull up my deepest secrets and feelings about my family and myself. But we just did endless exercises with numbers and words.

Dr. Ogilvy was a rather short man with a large waist, bald with short curly hair in two crescents over his ears. He was dressed in a shirt and tie, but had no jacket and carried a pad of paper with him to the stand. He already had sweat stains visible around his armpits.

Morales tried to swear the doctor in as an expert witness, but David asked to "voir dire"" him, or rather, ask him first about his credentials. This was done outside the hearing of the jury, which was excused to the adjacent jury room.

As it turned out, the doctor had evaluated over 50 criminal cases exclusively for the prosecutor's office. He has a psychology degree from an obscure university in the Dominican Republic and was not board-certified in psychology. He had not recently practiced psychology as a staff member in a hospital, health care setting or private practice nor published any professional articles, except for his blog.

The judge looked thoughtful after this description and decided to allow Dr. Ogilvy to be qualified as an expert, though she found that he just barely had the necessary credentials. However, the judge told David that he was free, on cross-examination, to point out any weaknesses in the doctor's background or expertise.

The jury came back in.

Morales stood before the witness. She asked him about his credentials, but knew enough not to probe too deeply. Morales only inquired about whether he had testified before in court and in what area he had a degree.

"Now doctor, did you have the opportunity to evaluate Mr. Quintana?"

"Yes."

"For what purpose?"

"Criminal responsibility and mental status."

"How long did you spend with Mr. Quintana?"

"About four hours."

This was an out and out lie and I felt like standing up and objecting myself. It was less than two hours before he rushed me out of his office like I was infected with a contagious disease.

"We performed an array of evaluative tests and talked at length."

We actually "talked" for about five minutes!

"Did you form any conclusions about Mr. Quintana's current state of mind?"

"Yes. My conclusion is that the defendant has traits and behaviors consistent with a sociopathic or psychopathic personality disorder."

"What do you mean by this?" Morales asked quizzically.

"Well, he does not appear to have a strong sense of what is morally correct or ethically appropriate, like most of us. He thinks in terms of what is good for him and what is not good for him. A sociopathic response to life's hurdles is whether or not he will be able to get away with something, not whether there is justification for prohibiting an activity.

"So, essentially, he knows the difference between right and wrong?"

"Correct. I don't mean to suggest that he can't understand society's rules and what constitutes a crime. He knows which of his actions are prohibited. He understands social mores. It's just that he doesn't feel restricted by them. He doesn't internalize them. If he can benefit from a self-serving act, and not risk punishment, he will do it with no remorse or regret."

"Now, doctor, regarding the events of April 10, did you have the opportunity to discuss these with him?"

"Indeed."

"What was your assessment of his ability, at the time, to understand what he was doing?"

"That he was aware of what he was doing, that he understood it to be a crime."

"But he did it anyway?"

Dr. Ogilvy nodded vigorously.

"Yes. Perhaps he thought it would be looked at as self-defense and he could get away with it. He certainly wouldn't have refrained from the shooting due to any conscientious objections. Sociopaths do not have a conscience and can't empathize with others. I mean, look, he obviously didn't stick around to see if the victim was all right after he shot him. Or call the police to report it. Doesn't that suggest lack of empathy?

"OBJECTION!" Daniel shouted forcefully. "Speculative. The witness is making unsupportable assumptions about claimant's motives."

"Sustained. The jury will disregard the witness's last statement."

Morales nodded, rolling her eyes ever slightly.

"What is your opinion about Mr. Quintana's contention that he could not remember the event and had a period of temporary insanity if you will?"

"I think that is PREPOSTEROUS."

Dr. Ogilvy was enjoying himself. He leaned back and smiled at his use of the word "preposterous" and said it slowly and distinctly, for emphasis. I doubt if all of the jurors even understood this word.

"Why do you say that?" Morales tilted her head innocently.

"Nothing in my evaluation indicated that Mr. Quintana has any history of a fugue state, which is a short period of memory loss. I saw nothing to indicate that Mr. Quintana was ever unable to control his own actions."

"What about the idea that he was protecting his dog? That faced with his dog being in danger, he became emotionally overwrought and out of control?"

"The dog was his property and the victim was threatening his property. Obviously that made him angry. I doubt he cares all that much about a dog. No more than he is able to form real attachments to people … "

"So, your conclusion about claimant's criminal responsibility is what?"

Ogilvy sat up in his chair and raised his voice.

"That Mr. Quintana knew what he was doing when he shot Mr. Pruitt and knew that what he was doing was prohibited by law."

Morales nodded at her witness and looked at me briefly, as if she now knew how horribly dangerous I was.

"Nothing further for this witness."

David gathered up his notes. He sighed and frowned as he looked at Dr. Ogilvy before approaching him. On cross, David was able to get the doctor to admit that he graduated from a school in the Dominican Republic, that he had had privileges at only two rural New Mexico hospitals in the past and these had been suspended. He got the doctor to admit that his primary work was as a consultant for the prosecutor's office and he had ceased seeing private patients more than five years ago. The good doctor admitted that his license was yanked from the state of Idaho ten years earlier due to questions of Medicaid fraud.

I thought that this was a good start. Dr. Ogilvy's armpit stains were expanding.

"Now, Doctor, did you have a chance to evaluate Mr. Quintana's medical records before your evaluation?"

"No. None were given to me."

"Did the prosecutor's office give you ANY records to review prior to your evaluation?"

"No. They did not."

David looked incredulously at Morales and then the jury. I could see Morales was furious because there really hadn't been any medical records to provide.

"And you said you spent about four hours completing your evaluation."

"Yes. That is correct."

"If I produced a witness who would testify under oath that Mr. Quintana went into your office and came out in less than TWO hours, would you say that statement would be a lie?"

Ogilvy made a face and tilted his head, trying to figure out, I imagine, if David was bluffing.

"I thought it was about four hours."

"Would you please answer my question."

"Umm ... well ... I suppose it could have been two hours. I wasn't checking my watch. I was talking to the subject. I did spend some time working on my notes after he left."

"Well, you told the prosecutor that the EXAMINATION took four hours. Now you are saying that the examination may have been two hours, and you may have used the next two hours to review your notes. Is that correct?"

"Well ... possibly ... "

"OK. During the course of this examination, you stated that you performed the WAIS-R Intelligence Test, the Proverbs Test and the Serial Numbers Test. Is that correct?

"They are important criteria for determining ...

"Doctor. I asked you if those were the tests you administered. Yes or no?!"

"Yes." The doctor started to turn red, his confident voice suddenly diminished a bit.

"Now, please explain how many questions are involved in the WAIS-R?"

I believe it is about 80.

"And the Proverbs?"

"That is about 40 questions."

"And the Serial Numbers Assessment?"

"About 30 questions."

David squinted as if he was making important mathematical calculations.

"Ok. After your introductions, you asked Mr. Quintana almost 150 formalized questions, each one involving reading the question, the subject thinking about it and you recording the answer in your notes. Could you actually do this in two hours and still have time for a lengthy interview?"

"Well, I am very efficient."

"Even if you were faster than a speeding bullet, two hours would be the absolute MINIMUM time necessary to ask all these questions, wouldn't you agree?"

The witness looked very confused, his head turning side to side, and he closed his eyes and pretended to do calculations.

"It is entirely likely that it could take that long, yes. Possible."

"Thank you."

"Now, what can you determine from these tests you performed over the course of your two hours with Mr. Quintana?"

The doctor sat up in his chair, smiled and appeared relieved and revived. A question he was prepared to answer.

"Basic intelligence, verbal abilities, computational abilities, receptive and expressive language skills, psychotic thought processes … "

"Ok. What about Mr. Quintana's intelligence?"

"Well, above average intelligence. He rated quite high on verbal abilities and his performance scores were only a little lower."

"Any psychotic thought processes?"

"None that I could detect."

"Any mood disorders."

"He did appear a bit depressed and anxious."

"Wouldn't this also be normal for a subject accused of murder and facing the rest of his life in jail?"

"Yes, I suppose. I really don't know him that well."

"So true." David slipped in this comment quickly before asking his next question, leaving Morales no time to object.

"So, Mr. Quintana did not have any scores that rated unusually abnormal?"

"No, but … "

"And given what you just testified to under oath, you didn't even have time to converse with Mr. Quintana except in the form of asking quantitative test questions?"

"I'm not sure that … "

Are you acquainted with the Diagnostic and Statistical Manual of Mental Disorders, 4th edition?"

"Yes."

"And is it generally accepted as the leading authority on diagnosis and treatment of mental illnesses?"

"Yes it is."

"Well according to the DSM, sociopathy or psychopathology are difficult to assess with the tests you administered. Wouldn't you agree?"

"Generally, yes … but I also used the proverbs test …"

"Ah! Yes. *'The Proverbs Test,'* " David said sarcastically. By asking claimant to interpret common proverbs, you can determine that he is a psychopath?"

"They are helpful in making such an assessment, yes."

David went through each of the questions in the proverbs tests used to assess psychopathic tendencies and it appeared my answers were no different than that of most people. -

Dr. Ogilvy stuttered uncomfortably … "but one has to read between the lines … "

"You mean you have to have the expertise to see things that aren't really there … ?"

"No, that's not what I mean."

"Dr. Ogilvy, in how many cases have you been called to testify for the prosecution as an 'independent' expert?"

"I don't recall exactly."

"Well, I show here, through my research of court records, that it has been 53 times. Would that be accurate?"

"Yes. I suppose so. I haven't … "

"And in how many of these cases did you end up finding for the prosecution instead of for the defendant?"

"I don't think … "

"All of them. All 53 of them. Am I correct, doctor?

"If I could explain … "

"Would your answer be 'yes'?"

"Yes," the doctor said weakly.

"And you are paid by the prosecutor for your testimony in each case, correct?"

"Um … well, yes."

Daniel turned to the judge. "I have nothing further at this time."

The judge, who had appeared very interested in the exchange between David and Dr. Ogilvy, slowly turned her attention from the verbal flagellation of the doctor to the prosecutor.

"Any redirect, Ms. Morales?"

Morales, who was whispering hurriedly with her assistants, turned to her notes and started flipping through them quickly.

The judge leaned forward.

"Ms. Morales?"

I knew from watching television legal dramas that a lawyer should never ask questions of a witness to which she does not already know the answer. Apparently, Morales was smart enough not to try to "rehabilitate" this witness—what lawyers call trying to prop up a witness's damaged credibility (as you can see, I have certainly learned a lot of legal terminology over the past year!).

Morales put down her notes, sighed and said, "Not at this time your honor. But I would like to reserve the right to call the doctor as a rebuttal witness."

The judge couldn't resist. "THIS witness, counsel?"

"Uh. Yes, judge."

"Alright then. Dr. Ogilvy, you will please stay outside the courtroom should Ms. Morales wish to again call you as a witness."

"Any further witnesses?"

"Um … I call Janet Trujillo."

David had told me that Janet Trujillo was an employee of the veterinarian's office and was most likely called to testify that I was not in a state of panic or mental collapse when I brought in Lupe after the shooting. She would support Morales' theory that, because I wasn't acting crazy, I couldn't have been temporarily insane around the time of the shooting.

Janet Trujllo was a thin woman of about 25, with pinkish streaks running down the length of her short brown hair. She had come to Court attired entirely in maroon. I recognized her as the desk clerk who had helped me that night, the night of the shooting.

The witness was seated, and Morales approached.

"Now Ms. Trujillo, what is your occupation."

"I am a receptionist at the Rio Puerco Emergency Veterinary Clinic in Rio Rancho. I am currently studying for my vet tech's license."

"Thank you, but I really don't need to know your educational … " Morales quickly stopped, realizing she had morphed into her prosecutorial mode, forgetting for a moment that this was HER witness. She smiled.

"I wish you luck on your studies, of course. Now, what hours did you work on April 10?"

"I was working the 5 p.m. to midnight shift. We are an emergency 24-hour veterinary clinic."

"Yes. I know. Did you see Mr. Quintana come into clinic that evening?"

"Yes."

"About what time?"

"I would say about 6:30 p.m."

"Why did he come in?"

"He was carrying his dog with him. She was bleeding quite a bit … "

Morales interrupted. "Ms. Trujillo. Please. I just asked you WHY he came in."

Before David could object, the judge interrupted.

"The witness is explaining that, counsel. Go ahead Ms. Trujillo."

Janet Trujillo looked a bit perplexed by the squabbling. But she continued to explain that Lupe was bleeding quite a bit and the white sheet around her neck was red with blood.

Morales obviously did not want to have the jury sympathize with me or with the dog. So, she chose her next words carefully.

"Now, let's turn our attention to Mr. Quintana. At the time he came in, was he making sense?"

"What do you mean?"

"Did you understand what he was saying?"

"Why, yes."

"Did he seem like he was crazy?"

"OBJECTION," David yelled. "The witness is not an expert on mental health, your honor."

"Sustained."

"Ok, did he seem sensible in his request for assistance?"

"Yes. He wanted us to take care of his dog."

"After the dog was taken away, what did he do?"

The witness again looked confused.

"He sat in the waiting room?"

"For how long?"

"Hmm … About three or four hours. We had to take x-rays, it was kind of backed up that day … "

"Never mind about that," Morales interrupted impatiently. "During the time he was there, did Mr. Quintana do anything unusual?"

"Not really."

"Did he cry, scream, talk to himself or bother other people around the room."

"Not that I noticed. But I was busy. I didn't look at him all the time." She shrugged, "Maybe he did." She looked at Morales with a slight smile, like she had scored a small victory over her tormenter.

"When he left with his dog, did he seem okay?"

"Very, very relieved. Very happy. I could tell he loved her."

Morales knew she had to get rid of Janet Trujillo. She was volunteering far too much "unhelpful" information.

"Was there anything that would have made you nervous to be around him for the three or four hours you were in the same area together?"

"Not at all. He was a very polite man."

Thank you. Morales turned around quickly.

When David approached the witness, he had a smile on his face.

"Hello Ms. Trujillo."

"Hello." She smiled back.

"How long have you worked at the Rio Puerco Animal Clinic?"

"About two years."

"So, you have seen a lot of people come and go with their sick pets?"

"Oh, yes. Many. Hundreds probably!"

"And many of them that come in are facing life-threatening injuries or illnesses?"

"Yes. It's an emergency clinic," she again reminded the courtroom.

"Would you agree that most clients are worried when they bring in a seriously ill pet?"

"Yes. Of course."

"And Mr. Quintana was worried, wasn't he?"

"Yes, very worried."

"And scared?"

"Yes."

"How did he treat his dog?"

"Well, I do remember that he was very gentle with her, that he kept whispering in her ear, and kissing the top of her head."

"When she was taken away, you said he sat and waited?"

"Yes."

"Did he talk on his cell phone? Eat snacks? Talk to the other people in the waiting room?"

"No. He just sat down, looked at the floor with his hands clasped together and didn't really move at all."

"Didn't move for three or four hours?"

"Not that I saw. You know, now that I think of it, I do remember his leg was bouncing up and down though. Making a tapping sound on the floor. I remember that because the other girl there commented that it was like having a woodpecker in the room."

"What was he like when his dog was brought out to him?"

"I remember he looked so relieved. He could barely speak to the doctor, had tears in his eyes, just kept nodding his head."

"So, would you agree that you really couldn't tell what was going on in Mr. Quintana's head, except that he loved his dog."

"That's right. He was really worried."

"Thank you Ms. Trujillo."

I was somewhat confused about what Morales and David were trying to prove through Janet Trujillo's testimony. But David explained later that Morales was trying to show the jury that I was sane and rational around the time of the murder, not even temporarily off balance, and David was trying to show the jurors that I was deeply worried and even obsessed about Lupe's well-being, which would support the temporary insanity claim. I had some difficulty grasping these arguments and worried that the jury would be lost too.

Morales announced that she had no further witnesses, despite the fact that the entire police department and half the neighborhood was on her witness list. I think she felt the law was so obviously on her side, she didn't need to introduce any other witnesses to establish that I was a maniacal cold-blooded killer or an angry drunk. All she needed to show is that I killed someone to protect a dog. And that I wasn't "temporarily" insane at the time.

The judge announced she had an emergency in another courtroom and the trial would proceed the following morning with the defense putting on its case. I was very tired, very confused by the whole process, tired of the lies and of people talking about me, and just wanted to go home to see Lupe. I wanted to scratch her behind her ears, to just lie down on the couch with her, and not think of anything having to do with witnesses, objections and courtrooms.

Maria, David and I left quietly out the back door. I could sense that there was tension between David and Maria. They stood on either side of me and did not look at each other. I looked at Maria's face and she looked stonily at the ground. What was going on between them? I supposed that this trial was killing everyone's spirit. We marched down the back steps of the courthouse and to the car like we were proceeding to a funeral.

David shook my hand, patted my back and told me that everything was going well, in his fast "rat-a-tat" speaking style. I grasped his hand between mine and pulled him toward me. "She really likes you, you know" I whispered. David pulled back and looked at me with surprise. Then he raised his eyebrows and had a huge smile on his face. "I'm so glad to hear that, Anastasio!"

As we got into the car, Maria asked me what I had said to David.

"I said thank you. I told him that he has made me feel more confident."

Maria nodded "Oh. I'm glad. He is such a good lawyer. Top of his class." Her voice was weak.

On the way home, Maria stared out the window blankly. Within a short time, we were home and I could see Lupe's nose plastered against the front window. I couldn't help but smile at the goofy open-mouthed face wiping streaks of mucus across the glass.

Lupe came through the front door and leapt at me and then Maria, thrilled that we were all together again. I crouched and patted her on the head. Maria observed with an inscrutable look on her face, like disdain or even jealousy. I wished I could hug Maria and kiss her on the cheek for all that she was doing for me, but I just looked up and smiled weakly. This wall between us seemed impenetrable again. Didn't I have enough to think about right now that I didn't have to worry about her moods too? But as soon as this thought passed through my mind, I felt ashamed. And, again, so tired.

We had a quiet evening. I tried not to think about my trial and about what the jury might decide to do with me, but I was content for the moment sitting with Lupe on the back steps, watching the sunset, turning the mountainside different colors. I wished I could freeze the moment forever, never going forward, never going back.

Maria and I were quiet at dinner, discussing some of the moments at the trial, the foolishness of Cora, the stupidity of Dr. Ogilvy and the arrogance of the prosecutor. When I brought up David and how brilliant he was in cross-examination, Maria said "He really is a wonderful man." I looked at her quizzically, and she quickly added … "A wonderful lawyer, I mean, very skilled and confident. You are lucky to have him as your attorney."

So, Maria liked David. And David liked Maria. Yet, something was wrong. I wanted to ask Maria why she wasn't happy about finding someone she liked and respected, but old patterns and pressures rendered me mute. I knew from Raquel's conversations on the phone that Maria felt she would never get married, that she never WANTED to get married. Yet, I could tell she was very sad tonight, and not just about my trial. Maybe she couldn't trust men. Or couldn't trust herself to love someone. I wouldn't blame her, having had me as a father.

I remember when she had just entered high school, Maria developed a crush on a good-looking boy. I can't remember his name, but he was a typical low-life troublemaker. He was the opposite of Maria—he had poor grades, was absent frequently from classes, and seemed interested only in himself. Because of rumors circulating in the school that Maria liked him, and because she was so pretty, he asked her on a date and she accepted. I met him only once and he just stared at me for a moment, unsmiling, and said "Hey man" and kept smoking his cigarette.

After two or three dates, during which time her mother threatened to disown her, Maria revealed that the kid told her that she was boring, and if she wasn't going to "put out," he had no interest in her. Maria was crushed and I recall it took a week for her to stop pouting. I don't believe that Maria even really liked this boy and wondered at the time what in the world would drive a girl to desire someone who clearly didn't want her?

I went to bed soon after 9 p.m., feeling drained and empty. Lupe settled in, pressed against my back, her body heat quickly warming my spine.

She soon was snoring contentedly with an occasional twitch of the leg. I turned over onto my back and put my hand across her chest, feeling its slow and steady rise and fall.

Before I could fall asleep, I could hear Maria in her room, and she was crying. I got up quietly and crept to her door, which was cracked open. I saw her sitting on the edge of the bed, hunched over, weeping into her hands. My heart just broke. I leaned against the wall and the noise startled Maria. She looked up at me and we stared at each other for a moment, unable to move. Then she got up, nodded, said goodnight and closed her door. I just stood there, inches from the wood, and stared at the peeling white paint, feeling more helpless than I had in my entire life. I must have stayed there for ten minutes, wanting to comfort her, wanting to go to sleep, wanting to get into my truck and make a run for the border. But I finally turned around and went back to my bedroom. After sitting on the edge of the bed for several minutes, I finally knew what I could do to comfort my daughter. I motioned for Lupe to follow me, quietly opened Maria's door and then nodded my head for Lupe to go inside. Lupe looked me in the eyes for a second, cocked her head, and then to my surprise, went inside the darkened room and lay down on the bed beside my daughter. In a moment, I saw Maria move over to give Lupe more room.

Chapter 20

The next morning was unusually cloudy and gray. In New Mexico, you typically expect to see the turquoise blue sky covered only for a few minutes by some errant clouds. Today, however, it seemed as though an oceanic hurricane had traversed the desert, settling in for a long stay. "Was this a bad sign?" I wondered.

David and I were, once again, the first ones in the courtroom with Maria behind us in the front row of the spectator section. I smiled at David and patted him on the back, as he seemed more nervous than I was. David rearranged his notes, smiled weakly and nodded.

Soon, Judge Tsosie got the jurors in their seats and opened the courtroom for business. She then looked at David and asked him if he was ready to proceed. She glanced at me briefly with a neutral expression.

"Your honor, as my first witness, I would like to call Isidro Baca to the stand."

Morales jumped from her seat and objected loudly, claiming that the witness's testimony was irrelevant, an obvious attempt to bolster my character, not testify to the facts surrounding Pruitt's death.

David rose to respond, but Judge Tsosie held up her hand to him and thought for a moment. She called the lawyers to the bench. David filled me in later.

"Mr. Rubin, is that the primary purpose of this witness? To bolster Mr. Quintana's character?"

"Yes, your honor. To show that my client is NOT a violent man as the prosecution has repeatedly asserted."

The judge nodded and turned to Morales.

"Counselor, since you have attempted to paint Mr. Quintana as a violent and angry man as part of your prosecution, using your own witnesses to establish this, Mr. Quintana has the right to rehabilitate his reputation, also using witnesses. Your objection is overruled."

Morales went to her table, sighed loudly and sat.

Isidro was a former coworker of mine, at the plumbing business, whom I had known for more than 25 years. Isidro was about ten years younger than me, but we had always seemed to get along well at work.

After establishing how Isidro knew me and for how long, Daniel asked him about the kind of worker I was.

"Very good. Very hard worker," he responded. I had always enjoyed listening to Isidro's strong singsong New Mexico accent, where the last syllable of each sentence rises in pitch like it was a question.

"Tacho was always there on time and stayed late if someone asked him. Que no? He never slacked off."

"Did he get along with everyone at the company?"

"Well, he was actually sort of a loner. He kept to himself most of the time. He liked to take a book out back and read during lunch hour … We used to tease him about being a librarian when he grew up. He would just smile back. He was a quiet guy."

"Did he ever get in fights with anyone?"

"Oh, no … he minded his own business."

"Did you ever see him come in drunk?"

"Well … I would see him looking like hell some mornings. You know, his eyes all bloodshot and face kind of pale. Everyone knew that he drank."

"A lot?"

"Quite a bit, I think."

"But he would still come to work?"

"Uh huh. And even when he didn't feel well … I could tell when he didn't feel well … he always did his job anyway."

"Did he ever talk about his family?"

"Hmm … almost never. Of course, in San Sebastian everyone knows everyone else more or less. So, we knew about his family. There were … troubles."

"Did he ever talk about his next door neighbor, Wendell Pruitt?"

"Once in awhile, he would tell us that these motorcycle gang freaks had a wild party and threw beer bottles all over his yard and scared his wife.

Morales was up. "Objection to the term motorcycle freaks … "

"Overruled." The judge turned to Morales using her grade school teacher's voice.

"The witness isn't claiming to know anything about these people. He is simply recalling his conversation with Mr. Quintana at the time. To show state of mind."

Morales sat down.

David resumed. "Did he get upset at anything else about his neighbor?"

"The guys there would whistle at his wife when she was in the yard. He was really upset about that."

"Did he ever threaten to hurt Pruitt?"

"No, not that I ever heard."

"Have you ever known Mr. Quintana to hit or strike anyone?"

"No. I can't remember him ever doing that."

"And you have known him for over 25 years, correct?"

"Yes, I saw him almost every day."

David thanked Isidro, and Morales had her turn.

"Now, Mr. Baca. You said that Mr. Quintana was a habitual drunk."

"No, I didn't."

"Well, you said he often drank and came to work hungover."

"I have to admit, on more than one occasion, I have done the same thing." The courtroom broke into laughter.

Morales did not smile.

"But you knew that Mr. Quintana drank?"

"Yes, I said that."

"Isn't it true that Mr. Quintana was suspended once at work for coming to work drunk."

Isidro thought for a moment and then said, "Nah. That isn't true."

"Well, I have his employment records right here. It says that he was suspended for coming to work inebriated."

"When was that?"

Morales snapped. "You answer the questions and I'll ask them."

Isidro gave her a hard stare.

"I think it was a long time ago. I actually think he had the flu, was vomiting, que no? And the boss thought he was drunk."

"So, you are questioning the observations of your own boss?"

"Yeah. I sure am. He was a "pendejo." There was more laughter from the courtroom.

Morales realized she wasn't getting anywhere. She glanced at her notes.

"Let's turn to Mr. Quintana's history of violence. You don't remember Mr. Quintana shoving a Mr. Raul Uribe against the wall in January of 2005?"

Isidro's eyes opened wide.

"Oh, yeah. I remember that. I remember that one well."

Morales smiled.

"So, Mr. Quintana DID engage in violent behavior toward other workers after all." She looked triumphant.

"Well, maybe he did that day. That stinker Uribe thought he was alone in the front office, and tried to stick his hand under the dress of one of the secretaries, Tara Morales. She screamed and Tacho came in and pushed the guy against the wall. Uribe was fired on the spot."

"But you didn't see that happen?"

"No, but Tara told me about it later."

"OBJECTION," Morales asserted. "Hearsay."

"Overruled."

Morales looked deflated.

"So, Mr. Baca, despite what you said earlier, Mr. Quintana HAS acted aggressively toward another?"

"What kind of man would he be if he hadn't?"

Morales rubbed her eyes briefly, looked at her notes and then ended her questioning.

The judge, her expression unreadable, watched Morales return to her table.

She turned to David.

"Next witness?"

David stood.

"I would like to call Hortensia Vigil."

Hortensia Vigil lived on the south side of Wendell Pruitt's house. He actually saved his best insults and garbage throwing for her yard since she called the police almost every day. Hortensia was elderly, about 80, with short white hair, very slim and small but, oddly carrying a very loud and deep voice. We often joked that all her growth hormones had been funneled into her vocal cords.

She took the stand and adjusted her sweater comfortably around her shoulders.

"Hello Ms. Vigil, David began. Could you tell us where you live?"

"At 345 Montebello Road, in San Sebastian."

"Did you live near a Mr. Wendell Pruitt?"

"Yes. Next door. For two horrible years."

"Now. Given your answer, I must ask you, you didn't like Mr. Pruitt and his guests, did you?"

"OBJECTION. Leading the witness."

The judge looked at Morales sternly, knowing the objection was silly, but she also knew she was right.

"Sustained. Mr. Goldman, please do not ask leading questions" she said in a soft monotone.

David tried again, inquiring about Hortensia's feelings about this neighbor.

"Oh, he was awful. Just awful. Noise at all times of the night, music, motorcycles, screaming. They would throw garbage over my fence. I think someone once threw human … waste over into my yard." She shook her head quickly trying to dispel the memory. "We, my husband and I, couldn't get a good night's sleep!"

"Did you ever have words with Mr. Pruitt?"

"Yes, I asked him to stop or I'd call the police. He and his friends would mock me, laugh at me and, once when he was in an upstairs bedroom looking out, he saw me looking at him from my room….and he pulled down his pants!"

Hortensia closed her eyes tightly, remembering this traumatic encounter.

"Did you ever call the police?"

"All the time. I called and called. Over and over."

"What happened?"

"Well, at first, they would come over and warn him. Then things would be okay for a day or two. Later, they started ticketing him, and actually brought him to jail for a week or so. But he would always come back, and his friends were always hanging around. After a month or so, the police would promise to come back and they never did. One stupid officer told me to move if I didn't like it. Now why should I move if they are doing all the bad things?!"

"So, you kind of gave up on the police after awhile?"

"What was the point? My poor husband died of a stroke a few years ago and I moved my bedroom into the other side of the house. I went to stay at my daughter's house a lot too."

"Did you form an opinion as to what kind of man you thought Mr. Pruitt was?"

"OBJECTION. This witness isn't an expert at categorizing the personality of human beings. She doesn't have the ability to determine … "

"Overruled," the judge spoke over Morales. "The witness isn't providing a personality inventory, Ms. Morales. She is offering her lay opinion. You can answer the question, Ms. Vigil."

David, who had wandered over to the defense table, leaned over and whispered to me that, with Judge Tsosie presiding, he never needed to defend his line of questioning when there was an objection.

David asked the question again.

"He was evil," Hortensia said scowling. "There was nothing good about the guy. When my husband died, he and his pals looked at the body being taken away and just waved, blew kisses and laughed. He was a monster … "

"Thank you, Ms. Vigil."

Morales approached Hortensia cautiously. This frail looking old lady had to be handled gently as the jury would probably look unfavorably to a massacre of their "mother" or "grandmother."

"Now Ms. Vigil," she smiled, "You called the police when you were upset with Mr. Pruitt, correct?"

"A lot of good that did!"

"Just answer the question, please."

"Well, yes, for awhile."

"Did your husband own a gun?"

"Yes."

"Did you ever contemplate taking the law into your own hands?"

"What do you mean?"

"Did you ever get so frustrated and angry at Mr. Pruitt that you considered shooting him?"

"What! Are you crazy?"

"No more questions."

Morales smiled and sat down, proud of her small victory.

But Hortensia wasn't done. She raised her low scratchy voice and yelled, "But I'm sure as hell happy that Tacho had the nerve to do it!"

"OBJECTION!" Morales yelled, but she was drowned out by the laughter in the courtroom.

"Sustained." The judge leaned over to Hortensia and wagged her finger. Hortensia just smiled and apologized for her outburst.

I knew that David's next witness was going to be Dr. Ortiz, the psychiatrist who had examined me. David told me what she was going to say and I had initially asked him if her testimony was absolutely necessary. As someone who had guarded his privacy so intently and for so long, I felt embarrassed at the thought of being dissected in open court. But David convinced me it was important, critical even, and I relented. If the choice was between being labeled crazy and walking free, or being deemed sane and sent to prison, I figured I could live more easily with the former.

"Next witness, Dr. Melanie Ortiz."

Dr. Ortiz rose, with the same serene and confident manner I remember from my interview with her. She approached the witness stand like she was balancing a book on the top of her head. Eyes forward, chin up. Definitely an "I'm not afraid of lawyers" expression on her face. I relaxed a little.

David had Dr. Ortiz explain her education (Stanford Medical School!), training, publications and board certifications and asked that she be qualified as an expert witness. Morales was given the opportunity to ask questions about the doctor's background before the judge ruled whether she was qualified as an expert witness. Ortiz looked at Morales right in the eye, leaned forward and raised her eyebrows in a "bring it on, sister" kind of way. Recognizing that she might have been outmatched in a battle over credentials, Morales hesitated and then said softly, "No objection."

"Then I will qualify Dr. Ortiz as an expert witness in the field of forensic psychiatry," the judge said.

David began his examination gently, giving the jurors an idea of the setting in which we met, the length of time we talked and what we discussed.

"So, Dr. Ortiz, did you have the opportunity to form an opinion about Mr. Quintana's mental status prior to and after the alleged incident?"

"Yes, I did. Mr. Quintana was clearly able to make rational decisions before the incident and after it. He does not have any type of chronic psychosis, dissociation or irrational thought processes."

"Did you form an opinion about claimant's mental health as a whole."

Yes, I did. Given Mr. Quintana's personal history, I would say that he has suffered from moderate but chronic post-traumatic stress disorder following early childhood abuse by his parents.

The courtroom became hushed. Expecting dry psychobabble, the jurors and audience members were suddenly jolted to attention after hearing the juicy words "early childhood abuse." All eyes were now on the doctor.

"Could you explain?"

"Mr. Quintana's parents were very strict with him, but did not counterbalance the harshness with kindness, protectiveness or respect. He was treated as a, I must say this, kind of *servant*, expected to do what he was told, punished severely if he did not. He not only received no unconditional love, but, essentially, no love at all."

"Why do you say this? Can you give examples?"

"Yes. Mr. Quintana told me that he was sometimes locked out of the house, even in winter, if he did something like leave the lights on or forget to flush the toilet. He told me he had spent some nights in the tool shed wrapped in a tarp for warmth. His parents fought with each other frequently and violence was common between them. They then acted violently towards the children as well. Mr. Quintana was hit with a metal belt buckle in the face by his father, giving him a scar above his eye …

The doctor pointed to the area above her left eyebrow. The jury turned to me as one to try to see the mark on my forehead.

The doctor continued.

"Mr. Quintana's mother slammed a mental tortilla pan on his hand when he tried to sneak a bit of food from the stove. He fractured three fingers. This was apparently a daily event in that house. One child, an older sister, was apparently raped, got pregnant as a result, and was thrown out of the house in the middle of the night."

"How did Mr. Quintana deal with all this?"

"He retreated into himself. He hid his emotions, he avoided contact with other people, he confided in no one and later took to drinking to deal with his loneliness and isolation."

"What about his wife and daughter? He had them for support, didn't he?"

"Apparently, Mr. Quintana retreated further within himself emotionally shortly after the marriage. When his wife became vocally disapproving of his behavior and his role as provider, he emotionally abandoned the marriage, seeing himself once again as a failure. He told me that he and his deceased wife rarely talked to each other in later years of their marriage."

The doctor thought for a moment.

"Regarding his daughter, Mr. Quintana said he loved her … LOVES her … tremendously and completely, but thinks he has always been a disappointment to her. He ended up avoiding her when she was a child and later as an adult as a way of mitigating the pain of failing her. He couldn't stand the idea that she might be ashamed of him, or embarrassed by him."

I started to tremble, hearing all this painful history dredged up in open court. I looked at the table, squeezed my fists tight and tried not to cry. I was afraid to even turn my head for fear of seeing Maria's expression. I could only imagine how she was feeling right now. In additional to being a drunk, a killer and a bad husband, I was also a weak, spineless, useless father. And now everyone knew.

The doctor went on in her calm focused voice.

"Mr. Quintana has lived his life in hiding, from the community, from his family and from himself. He has felt as though he is worthy of no one's love and is incapable of expressing love himself."

David approached the doctor.

"What about his dog, Lupe?"

Dr. Ortiz relaxed a bit and smiled.

"Ah. Lupe. A most amazing story, actually. When Mr. Quintana rescued the dog from near death, he realized that she was completely dependent on him and it was necessary for him to care for her. Subconsciously, I believe, he desperately wanted to nurture someone, to offer protection and love. And, when he offered love to the dog, to his surprise, the dog responded. Instead of his being a disappointment and a failure, she appreciated his devotion to her, didn't examine any of his faults and simply wanted to be with him. This was the unconditional love Mr. Quintana never had. All the years of loneliness, of desperate need for connection, of bottled-up anger, made way for a thin stream of hope. Through this dog … Lupe."

"Why did he identify so closely with a dog? I mean, after all, she isn't a *'person.'* David looked over at Morales, mocking her with her own words.

"Well, Lupe's life was a mirror of Mr. Quintana's. His love had been rejected and he had been abused. Lupe was mistreated, beaten and ignored and finally left for dead. I think he saw the connection, that they were kindred souls. His realization was that Lupe had only Mr. Quintana to count on and he was not going to let her down. If he did, he knew he would be destroying himself."

The doctor nodded her head slightly, thinking of how to frame her next words.

"I believe that this was, or he believed it was … his last chance at redemption, if you will."

The jury was caught up in the doctor's wonderful descriptions, her fluid voice and her apparent sincerity and warmth. I notice when I finally looked up, that the jury was looking at me with much kinder expressions than they had before.

"Okay doctor. Let's get to the day in question. The one at issue in this trial." David tried everything not to say murder, killing or death.

"You mean the day Mr. Pruitt was shot?" the doctor asked.

"Yes, doctor," David replied sheepishly.

The doctor resettled herself in the chair and readjusted her brightly colored silk shawl around her shoulder.

"Well, when Mr. Quintana said he saw Mr. Pruitt with Lupe, holding a knife to her throat … "

"OBJECTION!," Morales roared. "There is no evidence presented that this actually happened. It is, at best, speculation."

The judge, also immersed in the doctor's testimony, looked shocked at this rude interruption. She turned to Morales.

"There is no evidence that that it did not happen. This testimony is not for the purpose of establishing who did what to whom, but simply a means to try to establish Mr. Quintana's state of mind. Your objection is overruled."

Judge Tsosie turned back to the doctor. "Please continue."

The doctor looked appreciatively at the judge. Everyone suddenly seemed to be rooting for me. Morales noticed this turn of tide and looked miserable sitting at her table.

"As I was saying, Mr. Quintana said he saw Mr. Pruitt holding a knife to Lupe's throat, sitting in his yard, laughing and threatening to hurt the dog. As you might imagine, Mr. Quintana felt rather helpless. Here is the dog he saved from mortal danger and he is impotent, he can't help her. Mr. Quintana pled with Mr. Pruitt to return the dog, but when Mr. Pruitt would not, and he said he would enjoy killing the dog, Mr. Quintana had what we psychiatrists call a 'dissociative break.' If he did not save the dog, he would have failed the only living creature that he saw as loving and needing him. And without Lupe's love, Mr. Quintana saw himself as doomed. Every last bit of hope and dread was wrapped up in this brief moment. Either Mr. Quintana acted or he was dead."

Dr. Ortiz glanced briefly at me.

"So, after he saw Mr. Pruitt had actually injured the dog, he entered a 'fugue state,' a period where his conscious thoughts were suspended. Then, his subconscious mind did what it thought he needed to do and couldn't do consciously … shoot Mr. Pruitt. Once the dog was safe, he was able to restore his sense of reality. He dropped the gun in the grass and went to the veterinarian.

"So, doctor, do you think Mr. Quintana understood what he was doing at the moment he shot Mr. Pruitt?"

No, I don't. I don't think he was thinking rationally or with any type of conscious thought process during that short window of time. I think he also suffered from residual confusion for some time afterwards, which would be expected. He said, for example, he was surprised to find the police at his house when he returned from the animal hospital."

"Would you call this 'temporary insanity'?"

"Well, I don't think Mr. Quintana has ever been insane, and I personally do not use this term clinically, but yes, he did not comprehend the consequences of his actions or that what he was doing was wrong. His action was a raw survival impulse, separate and apart from conscious and rational thought. I believe the law labels this as 'temporary insanity'."

"Is that different than acting out of extreme anger or rage?"

"Most certainly. The extraordinary fear in that moment the dog was injured triggered Mr. Quintana's subconscious to seize control ... the way an abused child will sometimes become uncommunicative and catatonic during an attack or even develop an alternate personality to deal with unbearable pain. When suffering is too great to bear, an assault on the psyche too great, some people, in some circumstances, will simply lose their free will. Their base instinct takes over for self-preservation. This is what happened to Mr. Quintana, in my opinion."

"But Mr. Quintana knew how to aim and fire the gun ... "

"Yes, the way a person with multiple personalities will be able to cook a gourmet meal or paint a beautiful portrait, while completely unaware of doing so. This process of dissociation doesn't mean that one doesn't know HOW to act, it means that one can't control the action or remember it."

"I see. Then wouldn't this mean that Mr. Quintana remains a danger to others if he has this personality trait?"

David told me that, while this wasn't an issue at the trial—whether I might be at risk of re-offending—he felt this was a question the jury would most certainly have in the back of their minds.

"Well, it's not a personality trait. And it is extremely unlikely that the same scenario would present itself again. In my professional opinion, this was a one-time occurrence, it never happened before, and it almost certainly would never happen again."

"Are you familiar with the state of New Mexico's definition of criminal responsibility?"

"Yes. It was part of my training. I was asked to perform a criminal responsibility assessment in this case—that is, whether Mr. Quintana's actions or state of mind fit or did not fit the state's definition of being responsible criminally for his behavior."

"So, Doctor, in your opinion, was Mr. Quintana criminally responsible for the death of Wendell Pruitt?"

"No."

"Why did you reach that conclusion?"

"In order to be criminally responsible, one would have to understand the nature and consequences of his actions … that what he was doing was wrong. There is no question in my mind that, at the time of the shooting, Mr. Quintana was not in control of his actions, did not comprehend the nature of his actions at the time, and was unable to assess whether his actions were wrong. He is not criminally responsible in my opinion."

David thanked Dr. Ortiz and sat down, a bead of sweat trickling down the side of his head, just in front of his ear. He looked me in the eyes, and then nodded reassuringly. I amazed myself at what I did next. I put my hand on top of his for a moment … felt the warmth of his hand, and then withdrew. I hoped he was not offended.

Morales was up next. As the prosecutor approached the witness for cross-examination, the doctor eyed her casually, but did not appear fearful in any way. Morales smiled at Dr. Ortiz and thanked her for her presence in court.

Pleasantries aside, Morales appeared eager to attack, like a hungry hyena stalking its prey. She circled in front of the jury, deep in thought, tapping her chin dramatically with her forefinger before returning to the witness stand.

"Dr. Ortiz, how long did you meet with Mr. Quintana for your evaluation?"

"About two hours."

"Two hours. Just two hours. Yet, you seem to know everything there is about his past and his personality and his character and his family. Did you learn all this in two hours?"

"Yes, I did." Ortiz was firm.

"But you said that, at first, Mr. Quintana had difficulty opening up to you."

"Yes. But I explained it was in his best interest to be forthright and honest."

"How long before he started to 'open up'?"

"Perhaps ten minutes."

"So, you had only an hour and fifty minutes, approximately, to learn his life story?"

"Yes. That's about right." Morales pretended to be surprised at this response.

"A little over an hour and a half. Okay. Wouldn't you agree that Mr. Quintana is a smart man?"

"Yes, I would. I believe he is quite intelligent."

"And he **now** understands the charges against him, the wrongfulness of his actions and the penalties for those crimes?"

"Yes."

"He is competent to stand trial?"

"Oh, yes."

"Yet, everything he told you, you simply accepted as the truth. Isn't it possible for a smart man, a well-read man, to fabricate a personal story in order to stay out of jail?"

"Yes, I suppose. But he wasn't."

And Morales made her first prosecutorial misstep, asking a question to which she didn't already know the answer.

"Well, how do you know that, doctor?"

"Through my training, my education, my thousands of hours of interviews with patients. I am very aware of the signs of manipulation, the body language, the verbal delivery and the small factual inconsistencies. I would call myself very well schooled in patient fabrication."

Morales, unable to help herself, continued down this line of questioning.

"Well, wouldn't you agree that it is not IMPOSSIBLE for someone to be able to ... how do I put it ... put one over on you?"

"Not impossible." Dr. Ortiz paused. "But nearly so. I am convinced it didn't happen in this case."

Morales stared incredulously at the witness for a moment and then wisely decided to move on.

"Alright doctor. You have done research on dissociative acts premised on extreme emotional distress. Or, to put more simply for the jury, blackouts or the appearance of multiple personalities following extreme stress?"

"Well. Yes. When described very basically … "

"And these cases you've researched and participated in, they have all pertained to stressful events involving threats between people?"

"What do you mean?"

"Well, every study you have done that I have read concerned people reacting to some horrible event happening to themselves, their family members or to other people. Not to a dog, a cat, a bird or a hamster."

Morales smiled, glancing at the jury.

"That's correct."

"Well then, wouldn't you agree that there is a big difference between the emotional suffering occurring at the loss or injury of a father, mother, or child and that of a DOG?"

Morales was obviously persisting in getting the jury to see the absurdity of comparing people and dogs … the theme song of her prosecution.

"No. Not at all. Studies have actually been done showing clearly that more than half of American families rate their pet dog as the family member they like the most. People can be in love with any number of living things. Even inanimate objects. I once had a patient who took a year to rebuild a vintage convertible and loved his car so much, he became actively suicidal when it was stolen. It is the viewpoint of the subjects I care about, not society's expectations or values."

Morales frowned dramatically. "So, a threat against someone's … DOG … can drive a man to murder. That's what you are saying?"

"Yes. As we see in this case." The doctor spoke as if talking to an idiot.

Shaking her head as she looked at the jury, Morales then went to her desk and examined her notes briefly.

"Now doctor, you say that Mr. Quintana was unaware of what he was doing when he shot Mr. Pruitt."

"Yes."

"Well, isn't it true that he had the presence of mind, after his dog was allegedly put at risk of harm, to walk across the yard, enter his house, take a gun out of hiding, leave the house, cross the yard, and aim the gun at

Mr. Pruitt and shoot him in the head. Wouldn't you agree that that would not seem to reflect a hysterical reaction on Mr. Quintana's part?"

"I never said he had a hysterical reaction. The way you might see it on television is not how it actually happens." The doctor sighed and went on.

"Rather, under extreme duress, some people with traumatic histories suffer from a split of their conscious and subconscious minds. It is the way for the subconscious to **protect** the conscious mind. Mr. Quintana was under such severe stress watching his dog's life threatened, his subconscious mind took over and was able to get him to discharge his gun, without him consciously recognizing what he was doing. Sleepwalkers for example can prepare a five course meal or converse on the phone and not have any recall of it in the morning."

Morales squinted and frowned as she turned to look at the jury.

"Well, doctor, you could also assert that Mr. Quintana may have simply been so pissed off at Mr. Pruitt for taking something that wasn't his, for all the trouble he had posed in the past, that he just decided to. … get his gun and shoot him. We've seen it before.

"Is that a question?"

The judge interjected. "Ms. Morales, no speeches. Ask questions."

"Well then, couldn't Mr. Quintana have shot Mr. Pruitt just because he was so damn mad at the guy and was at the end of his rope?"

"No. I didn't get the sense from Mr. Quintana that he was angry, just terrified. And he had no history of violence. He usually retreated from aggression rather than confronted it."

"Ah. And Mr. Quintana was so terrified that he rescued his dog after shooting Mr. Pruitt, put it in the car, drove it to the veterinarian's office and brought it back home later. Doesn't sound like terror to me."

"Well, he isn't you, is he?"

Morales shouted an immediate "OJBECTION!" and asked the judge to order the witness to respond to her question.

The judge glared at Morales.

"Ms. Morales, I would be glad to have the court reporter repeat the last comment you made, but it was not a question. Move on. Objection overruled."

The audience tittered a bit at this interchange but shushed right away, eager to hear more from these battling women.

"What I mean to say, Ms. Morales, is that Mr. Quintana was thinking only of his dog and saving her life and, because he was so identified with her, it meant saving his OWN life. He was focused on Lupe, not Mr. Pruitt."

Morales leaned closer.

"ORRRRR … Mr. Quintana could have knowingly concocted this amnesia bit to cover up his crime."

Morales looked at the jury conspiratorially. It seemed to me that Morales was trying to plant ideas in the jurors' minds rather than actually elicit a response from the doctor.

To her credit, the doctor did not get riled. She remained ramrod straight in her chair with a slight tilt to her head as she listened.

"Well, Ms. Morales, he didn't hide his gun after the shooting, he dropped it on the lawn for anyone to see. That doesn't seem like a criminal mastermind. He didn't take cash and clothes and flee for the border. He ran to the veterinarian and actually came back home several hours later. He didn't pretend that Mr. Pruitt had been threatening his own life, which could have given him a much stronger alibi, especially since there were no witnesses. But he told the truth. This doesn't sound like someone trying to cover up a crime."

Morales was exasperated. David had once told me a smart and experienced attorney would cut her losses when faced with an unshakable witness, saving her closing arguments for the jury. But Morales persisted. She wanted to score at least one point.

"C'mon doctor, a clever man like Mr. Quintana, who likes to read and go to the library, who you said is very intelligent, could have made up this whole thing, the story of the dog, the lapse in consciousness as you call it, as a way to get rid of Mr. Pruitt without having to pay for the crime. I mean, there have been movies made with similar plots. Wouldn't you agree?" Dr. Ortiz pondered this for a moment. She leaned forward slightly and looked Morales straight in the eyes and said firmly,

"If Mr. Quintana did that, I will be the first to admit that it would be the most brilliant job of acting that I have ever seen.

I could see the jurors turning slowly to look at me. Probably to assess whether I was indeed a brilliant conman, capable of fooling a nationally renowned psychiatrist and figuring an ingenious and novel way to get away with murder. What they saw was a hunched-over, gaunt old man in an ill-fitting suit. I saw their faces slowly turning away. I think they had concluded that I was no more a criminal genius than I was a circus acrobat.

Morales took one last stab at Dr. Ortiz.

"So, if Mr. Quintana was back to his right mind immediately after shooting Wendell Pruitt, shouldn't he have been expected to call the police, get an ambulance, try to help the injured man? What kind of person leaves a possibly mortally wounded man to take a dog to the veterinarian?!" Morales raised her voice indignantly.

Dr. Ortiz, to her credit, remained calm.

"In Mr. Quintana's mind, Ms. Morales, Lupe's life was still in danger. She was limp, unresponsive, bleeding from her neck. His first thought was obviously to save the life of the dog he loved and needed. He was still in a state of abject fear, mind you, even though he could now control his actions. I believe he was still confused. I see nothing pathological or criminal about a person loving a companion animal so much that her life becomes his priority."

Morales had finally had enough. She returned to her seat and the doctor was dismissed with the judge's thanks. Dr. Ortiz left the courtroom with the same calm confident manner in which she had arrived.

The next witness was going to be the hardest of all for me to hear. I had been dreading it since the beginning of the trial.

David rose. "For the next witness your honor, the defense calls Maria Quintana."

I could hear Maria rising from her seat behind me and I watched as she walked calmly to the witness stand. She sat down and then looked directly at me and offered a slight smile.

The courtroom once again became very quiet.

David grinned as he approached her and asked her how she was related to me, where she lived, what she did for a living, her marital status and where she went to school. Then the questions got tougher.

"So, Ms. Quintana, you have, of course, known your father Anastasio Quintana your whole life?"

"Yes." Maria spoke firmly, obviously prepared and ready.

"How much time did you spend with your father as a child?"

"Every day at dinner, and usually at breakfast. Not much else."

"Where was he when he was not at home with you and your mother?"

"Well, working of course. And he liked to go to the library to read. Once in a while he would wander around the hardware store and chat with people … but he was very much a loner."

"When you did spend time with him, was he ever verbally abusive or physically abusive?"

"No. Never. He never said an angry word to me, never yelled at me or even threatened to punish me. He just seemed … uncomfortable … being around me."

"So, you never saw any violent tendencies or periods of angry outbursts?"

"No. Usually, when my mother yelled at him, which was often, he just left the house or went to the bedroom."

"Was he demonstrable in his love for you?"

Morales stood and loudly objected.

"What relevance does the witness's relationship with her father have to do with this case?!"

David turned to the judge who was looking to him expectantly.

"The prosecution has suggested over and over that my client may be an amazing conman, violent, short-tempered and manipulative, capable of plotting the perfect murder. I believe he has the right to present evidence showing this premise not be accurate."

The judge nodded. "I agree. Overruled. The witness may answer."

Morales sat down. David repeated the question.

"No. My father was not very physically affectionate with me. I was told by my relatives that he had liked to hold me as a small baby. As far back as I can remember, he always seemed afraid to be alone with me. Later on, as I got older, we just avoided each other."

"Do you know anything about your father's childhood?"

Maria nodded solemnly. "Yes. My mother had told me that he was very much abused by his parents. Hit, humiliated, yelled at. He was thrown out of the house at all times of day and night, even in winter for small things … not putting the spoons in the right place, knocking over a glass of water … "

"To your knowledge, did he ever get mad at his parents?"

"Just once, I was told. When they took away his dog when he was about eight years old. He said he wouldn't speak to them after that, no matter how badly he was punished. And, after awhile, I guess they didn't even seem to care, so long as he did what he was told."

"So, from your point of view, your father had problems expressing his feelings?"

"Yes. More than anyone I've ever known." Maria looked at me sadly and I stared back, feeling miserable. "I think he just does not really trust anyone … well, trust them not to hurt him. He thinks everyone believes he is a failure."

"Did any of this change recently?"

"Amazingly, yes. After he rescued his dog, Lupe. I remember that he phoned me the day after he found her, which was very unusual. The phone call I mean. And he told me all about her and how happy he was she was going to be all right. He sounded so wonderful, so energetic, so different than … than I remembered him."

"So, he became attached to his dog?"

"It was almost as if, for the first time in my father's life, he found … "

Maria looked down for a moment, tried to compose herself, and then raised her head again, her eyes filled with tears. She whispered," … that he found love."

At this, I put my head down on the table and quietly sobbed. David walked back to me and patted my back. I heard the judge ask if I was all right. I quickly pulled myself together and whispered to David that I was okay. I lifted my head and everyone in the courtroom, from the jurors to Morales, was staring at me. I clasped my hands together, looked at the table and said, "I am very sorry, your honor."

The judge answered softly.

"It's all right, Mr. Quintana. If you ever need a break, just speak with your attorney and we can let you have one."

"Thank you, your honor." I glanced quickly at her as I said this, not wanting to cry again.

"Nothing further," David said.

"Any questions for the witness, Ms. Morales?"

Morales, who would probably have been better off saying no, decided to have a go at Maria. Knowing Maria's temper, and how she hated Morales, I knew the prosecutor was making a mistake.

"Ms. Quintana, did I hear you say that your father was an alcoholic?"

"No. But he was."

"For how long?"

"As long as I can remember. Since I was a little girl. He told me that, after he adopted Lupe, he finally stopped drinking. Cold turkey." Maria said this proudly.

"Well, in your memory, did he ever come home drunk?"

"Yes. I saw him drunk at home a few times. But my mother would send me to my room. Mostly, he drank outside the house."

"Did you have any idea what he was doing when he was drunk?"

"No. My mother told me he sat around in his truck or behind the high school bleachers … usually alone."

"You don't know if he ever got into any fights?"

"No. But San Sebastian is a small town. If there was a fight in the evening, we'd all hear about it by morning."

Morales didn't expect this remark and was silent for a moment.

"But he COULD have had all sorts of drunken fights without you knowing it?"

"I never saw him with any bruises, black eyes or broken fingers … "

"Ms. Quintana, that doesn't mean … Ok. Let's move on. And you said he stopped drinking after he got his dog. Correct?"

"Yes."

"Well, how do you know that it's true?"

"He told me."

"But you didn't see him going through the DT's or go with him to an AA meeting. He could have stopped AFTER killing Mr. Pruitt."

"No. I believe him."

"Well. You didn't even live here when he claims he stopped drinking. So, as far as you know, he could have been getting all liquored up the night of the shooting?"

"Anything's possible, I suppose. But my father doesn't lie."

"But, given what you've told us here today, wouldn't it be fair to say that you hardly know your father?"

Maria hesitated. She looked at me for a moment.

"Well. Yes. In many ways, I guess that is true."

You could see Morales doing an imaginary fist pump in the air. But she couldn't resist asking another question.

"So, this alcoholic father, who ignored you as a child, that you hardly know … couldn't he have done things that you wouldn't expect? Like get drunk and angry enough to take revenge on a man who had made his life miserable, to take that man's life?"

Maria just looked at the prosecutor straight in the eye and with a calm strong voice said, "That, Ms. Morales, is simply absurd."

"No further questions for this witness." Morales turned and walked away without customarily thanking Maria for answering her questions.

Maria sat down behind me again, and I could hear her sigh audibly. I was relieved it was over, but the pain of failing her as a father struck me anew like a sharp dagger. My daughter. My only child. I had missed knowing her. I had missed loving her. I don't know what hurt me more, my guilt at having abandoned Maria or the regret that I hadn't had her in my life. The negative thoughts started streaming in. "What kind of man was I after all … how could she ever forgive me?"

The judge suspended the trial for lunch.

David and I had lunch in one of the empty rooms by the courtroom, and Maria made excuses and told us she had to run home to let Lupe out in the yard. I could tell she was shaken. Certainly by what was happening to me, but perhaps more by talking in front of a bunch of strangers about the family secrets she had probably never shared with anyone before.

I was not in the mood to talk either, but listened as David explained that there were no additional witnesses, and they were ready to present closing arguments. He assessed the case as having swung in my favor, due primarily to the testimony of Dr. Ortiz and the theatrics of Morales, who he assumed the jury hated at this point.

"But, Tacho, I have to tell you honestly, we could still lose. This case received lots of press, the jury is under a lot of pressure and the fact remains that someone is dead. Juries like to see someone pay for murders, even of someone like Wendell Pruitt."

I nodded and sat silently for a minute, digesting David's last remark. Then, turning to David, I sat up straight in my chair and felt a sudden wave of energy and defiance coursing through my body.

"David. I want to testify."

David suddenly looked at me with his eyes open wide. He tried to dissuade me, tell me about the risks, scare me with horror stories of past clients who had taken the stand and lost their cases. David told me that Morales would do her best to humiliate me, confuse me, and make me look like a fool who either doesn't know the difference between a human and a dog or an evil person who doesn't care. I hadn't talked this over with Maria … I wished I could force her to stay out of the courtroom when I testified so she could be spared any more embarrassment.

"Tacho, it can't do any good."

But I insisted. "David, I wish I could just sit here and hope that everything turns out fine. I have listened to all these people, even my own daughter, telling me who I am, what I have done wrong in life and what I believe. If I have to spend years, perhaps the rest of my life in prison for saving Lupe, I want to know that I at least explained my own story. I don't want to be painted as a killer, a crazy person, a saint or a victim. I want them to know that, while I have made mistakes in my life and don't really have much to be proud of, I have always been an honorable man."

David argued with me for some time, but I was adamant. I had to take the stand. My co-worker Isidro got up there to defend me, as did my neighbor Mrs. Vigil. My daughter was publicly humiliated trying to help me. It was about time that I had the guts to defend myself.

David looked sad.

"Well. It is your right, of course. But once you testify on direct, you have to answer the prosecution's questions too."

I nodded.

David told me we could request a continuance, or delay, to give us more time to prepare. I knew that I would lose my nerve if I didn't testify now. That Maria and David would convince me not to. I needed to do this. I refused to wait.

When we went into the courtroom and everyone got settled, the judge took the bench and asked David if he had any other witnesses. David looked at me, and I nodded. He sighed loudly.

"Your honor. My client, Anastasio Quintana, would like to take the stand."

The courtroom gasped in unison. Morales turned to her assistant and clearly mouthed "Oh My God!" The judge had to bang her gavel to restore quiet. I heard Maria in back of me saying, "No, Papi, No!", but I didn't turn around.

The judge turned to me, and with a steady voice, asked me if I was sure, letting me know that I didn't have to testify.

"I know, your honor. My lawyer has explained this to me. But I have to."

She looked at me a moment and then, with very knowing eyes, nodded. "I understand. Go ahead Mr. Rubin."

"The defense calls Anastasio Quintana."

All eyes were on me as I stiffly got up from the defense table and walked to the stand. I was sworn in and sat down. For the first time in my trial, I got to see the large crowd that was listening as my freedom, my life, hung in the balance. I quickly turned away and decided to focus my eyes only on David. I didn't look again at the people in the courtroom.

In all those mystery books I have read, it always says that when the defendant takes the stand, the courtroom becomes "hushed." I have to say that was pretty much true at my trial. A few coughs, some shuffling feet, but generally stony silence.

David rose from the defense table and approached me with a big smile. Yet, I could see in his eyes that he was scared. I suppose he had no reason to believe I would help my case, and neither did I. Yet, at the time, I naively believed I could not put myself in jeopardy by telling the truth. And, if I had not testified and then was convicted, I don't think I could have forgiven myself for being once again the typical Anastasio, fearful and mute. Perhaps Lupe had given me the strength I needed to do this.

"Please state your name for the record," David began.

"Anastasio Luis Quintana."

I then told David my age, my address and my education.

David turned away, walked a few steps, and then turned back to face me. I suppose part of being a litigator must be to create dramatic effect. Or maybe he hadn't had time to formulate questions and was thinking on his feet. Suddenly I felt terrible for putting David in this difficult position.

"Now, Mr. Quintana. Do you live alone?"

"Yes. Well … I don't live with any other people, just my dog. But my daughter is staying with me now. At least temporarily. She actually lives in Seattle … " I realized that I was rambling nervously and stopped when David glared at me with raised eyebrows.

"When you speak of your dog, you mean Lupe?"

"Yes."

"How long has she been with you?"

"About a year or so, I think."

"Could you tell us how you happened to get her?"

I saw Morales rising behind David, fully ready to hear her loud "Objection!" But I was startled nonetheless when it rang out.

"Ms. Morales?" The judge asked quietly.

"This line of questioning is completely irrelevant. The story of how Mr. Quintana got his dog has nothing to do with the case at hand … "

David turned to the judge.

"Your honor, this evidence is critical to establishing my client's thinking at the time of the alleged crime. How he felt about this dog is central to his defense. How he came to have this dog relates to how protective he felt about her … "

"So it goes to his state of mind?" the judge asked.

"Yes your honor."

"The state's objection is overruled."

Morales sat down loudly, scraping her chair across the floor.

I explained carefully how I had found Lupe, nursed her back to health, established a relationship with her and earned her trust.

"And how important is the dog to you, Mr. Quintana?" David asked softly.

I took a deep breath and felt tears come to my eyes. I hesitated for a moment … trying to find the right words.

"I guess she has become the most important thing in my life. We get to be together all the time, share each other's company. She is very … understanding," I said, unable to keep from smiling suddenly.

I immediately stopped grinning and composed myself, clearing my throat.

"I don't feel lonely when she's with me. She gives me … a sense of purpose, I guess you would say. A feeling that I am a better man than I thought I was. I also very much want her to have a happy life after the horrible one she must have had. "

I hesitated for a second and then said, "Dr. Ortiz was right, "We are … connected."

David looked at the jury for a moment.

"Would you say that Lupe has become like a member of your family?"

"Yes, of course."

"Now, do you remember what happened April 10?"

"Mostly."

"When did you first see Wendell Pruitt that day?"

"I had come back from a movie in the afternoon. Maybe around 3 or 3:30. I heard Lupe barking in the back yard … I guess the door was unlocked and she had nudged it open. I went out and saw him sitting in his backyard, near the fence."

"Where was Lupe?"

"I went toward his yard when I didn't see her and then I saw him holding her. By the neck … "

My heart started to beat faster as I recalled that horrible moment.

I explained how Pruitt had threatened to kill Lupe, how he put the knife blade against her throat. How she looked at me for help, her eyes rolling back in her head. I told David that I started to shake, to panic.

"I wanted to throw myself through the fence. But I couldn't move or he might hurt her."

"What did you do next?"

I sighed and in a shaky voice I explained.

"I went and got my gun out of the closet. I have never used it except in target practice. That was years ago. I could see that it was still loaded. I remember my hands and legs were shaking, but I took the gun and went back outside."

"Did you plan to shoot Wendell Pruitt?"

"No. No. I wanted to scare him. To make him let Lupe go."

"Did it work?"

"No. He just laughed at me. He kept squeezing her throat and making her scream. Or is it yelp?"

"And then … "

"Then he took the knife, put the point on her neck, just below her jaw, and pushed it in. I could see a dark trickle of blood on the blade and on Lupe's fur. She cried out."

"What happened next?"

I was silent for a moment. Finally, I took a deep breath.

"I don't remember."

There was soft whispering in the audience.

"What was the next thing you remember?"

"I can recall seeing him sitting slumped over in his lawn chair, blood on his face. I was so focused on Lupe, who was lying on the ground bleeding too. I recall running across the lawn with her in my arms, getting into my truck, driving down the highway. I remember I was shaking, my heart was pounding."

"Did you know where you were going?"

"Yes. To the animal hospital. Lupe was hurt, though I didn't know how badly. I tried to get there as quickly as I could. I thought she was going to die."

"You returned to your home afterwards. Why?"

"Where else would I go?"

"Did you remember what had happened earlier with Mr. Pruitt?"

"I remember my mind being very hazy. I knew, but it didn't feel real."

"When you returned, the police were there. What did you tell them?"

"That I remembered everything up until just after Pruitt put the knife into Lupe's throat. I told the police that the gun might be lying on the lawn somewhere. They had already found it."

"Did they ask you who killed him?"

"Yes. I told them that I must have."

"Why did you say that if you couldn't remember?"

"Well, I was there, he was there, I had a gun, he was dead. It started to all make sense."

"Have you ever had your memory of shooting him return?"

"No. I just don't remember … doing that."

"What was your concern at the time? That you were going to be arrested? Put in jail?"

"No, all I was thinking about was Lupe. I was praying that she was going to be alright."

David smiled and put his hand over mine. He looked relieved.

"Thank you Mr. Quintana. That must have been very difficult."

David walked back to the defense table and sat down. I suddenly felt very cold, alone and in danger.

"Ms. Morales, would you like to cross-examine this witness?"

Morales rose and looked directly at me as a hunter would after spotting a prize elk walk into firing range. Her glance was confident and cruel. I believe she had hoped fervently for this moment to come.

"Why yes, your honor," she said in a syrupy voice. "I most certainly would like to ask a few questions."

As she approached me, I noticed that Morales' eye was twitching. She rubbed it once or twice, but the twitch remained. It occurred to me that maybe Morales was as scared of me as I was of her. She checked her notes, then raised her head and moved toward me. I had never been so close to her before. She has beautiful skin. Red lipstick, dark brown eyes, a small mole on her chin. She studied me for a moment, perhaps expecting me to rub my hands together like Snidely Whiplash or Ted Bundy, or to have a challenging smirk on my face. I think the sight of a slight stooped old man, with a scared look in his eyes, threw her a bit off stride.

"Hello, Mr. Quintana. I am Erica Morales. I wanted to ask you a few questions about your relationship with the deceased, Wendell Pruitt. You testified that your wife, and you, had had words before with Mr. Pruitt. Wasn't there bad blood between you?"

Bad blood? I wasn't sure what she meant.

"Well, I guess we didn't like each other. He had no respect for us, or for the other neighbors, really."

"We're just talking about YOU here." Morales snapped. "So, YOU didn't like Wendell Pruitt, correct?"

"No I didn't."

"Did you secretly hope that he would move away?"

"Not so secretly." There was a brief moment of laughter in the audience.

"So, when Mr. Pruitt continued to do all these things that you say bothered you and your wife, how did that make you feel?"

"Frustrated. We did call the police numerous times. But it didn't seem to help."

"HOW frustrated did that make you feel?"

"Very frustrated."

"Angry?"

"Yes, I suppose."

"How did you manage that anger when there appeared to be no means to make the problem go away?"

"We stayed inside a lot. I tried to avoid coming in contact with him."

"Have you ever been angry at people you worked with?"

"I suppose."

"And, let me check here … " Morales pretended to check her notes. "Didn't you punch a co-worker once while at work?"

"No. I never punched him. I PUSHED him. My friend Isidro explained that. He was harassing one of our secretaries."

"Is that what you do when you get annoyed? You SHOVE people?" I think Morales was trying to provoke me to see if she could get me to explode.

"He had his hand … up … her skirt." I looked down modestly. "She was screaming for help. I guess you could say he was molesting her?"

"So, you came to her defense."

"Yes."

"Why didn't you call the police? Why not call the supervisor and report him? Why not warn him that he shouldn't be doing that to her?"

Was this woman for real? If a man from San Sebastian, or a woman for that matter, had just stood there and called the police instead of doing something right away to help, that person would have been labeled a coward. They would have been whispered about for the rest of their days.

"I didn't think there was time for that. He was hurting her."

"So, violence was the only means you had to stop him."

"I reacted. Hopefully, any of the guys at work would have done the same."

Morales looked at the judge.

"Objection to speculation about what 'the other guys would have done'."

The judge offered a small sympathetic smile to me.

"Sustained. Please strike that from the record. Mr. Quintana. You need to listen carefully to Ms. Morales' questions."

"Yes, your honor."

But I was starting to see where Morales was heading.

"Now, when you saw Mr. Pruitt holding your dog, you thought he was trying to hurt her … "

"He had a knife against her throat. I didn't just think he was trying to hurt her, I SAW him hurting her."

Morales hesitated.

"Yes, in any case, did you feel the same type of anger you had when you pushed your co-worker?"

"I don't know. I was more frightened than angry."

"So frightened that you went into the house, opened the closet, pulled out a gun and then went back to face Mr. Pruitt."

"Yes, I did that BECAUSE I was so frightened he would hurt my dog. And, yes, I was angry. I thought he was going to kill her."

Morales smiled.

"So, you could say that you have had a history of acting violently when you are angry?"

"OBJECTION!" David boomed. The prosecutor cannot put words into Mr. Quintana's mouth about what constitutes a history of anything. That is her conclusion, not his …

"Overruled, Mr. Rubin. Mr. Quintana can answer."

"No, I don't have a history of acting violently. In my entire life, I have never touched my wife in anger, never spanked my daughter, never even hit my dog with a newspaper … I am one of the least violent people I know."

"Objection," Morales shouted weakly. "The defendant won't respond to the question."

The judge leaned forward.

"Overruled. You wanted to ask the question, Ms. Morales, so you have to live with the answer to that question."

Morales pouted for a moment, pretending to check her notes.

"So, Mr. Quintana. You testified that you had a weapon in your house as protection?"

"Yes, there was a string of burglaries a few years ago on our street. I wanted to protect my family in case someone came in at night?"

"Did you ever use the gun before?"

"Just for shooting practice. Right after I bought it."

"And did you ever have a burglary?"

"No."

"Did you wife want the gun in the house?"

"I never told her about it."

"So, why didn't you get rid of the gun when you found you no longer needed it?"

"There was no reason to get rid of it. It was in a safe place. And I felt more comfortable knowing it was there. My neighborhood has still had its share of crime."

"So, having a loaded gun in your house, how did that make you feel?"

"I don't understand."

"Did that make you feel scared? Or did it make you feel braver, bolder, knowing you could kill someone if you needed to?"

"OBJECTION!" David shouted. Before he said anything else, the judge interjected.

"No need. Mr. Rubin. Sustained. Ms. Morales, you can make your arguments at the end of the trial, raising whatever theories you wish. But I won't allow this kind of 'question' of a witness."

"Yes, your honor." Morales squinted and frowned as if caught with her hand in the cookie jar.

"Now, Mr. Quintana, that brings us to the issue of your dog. I think you testified that this dog is very important to you."

"Yes. Very important."

"And you would do anything to protect her?"

"Within my power."

"Do you believe that she has the same rights as a human being would?"

"What?"

"OBJECTION!" David stood again. "This is irrelevant and immaterial and prejudicial!"

The judge looked at Morales.

"What is your response, Ms. Morales?"

"Well, it is clear that the defendant shot a human being in order to protect the health and life of an … animal. A dog. Which is illegal. I think it is relevant and material to discern how the defendant, Mr. Quintana, views the value of a dog's life … compared to that of a human."

The judge called the attorneys to the bench and I overheard the exchange.

"For what purpose do you need to ask this question?" the judge asked Morales.

"To show lack of willingness to offer a human being the respect for life that he is due. Because the LAW says a person's life is more valuable than a dog's, it is fair to ask if this is his view. It could show reckless disregard for human life … "

The judge closed her eyes and pondered this for a moment. She sent the lawyers back.

"Mr. Rubin, your objection is overruled. The witness may answer. But don't overstep, Ms. Morales … I'm listening carefully."

Morales came to stand in front of me.

"So, Mr. Quintana, is a person's life more important than a dog's?" Morales had a challenging tone and actually put her hand on her hip for emphasis.

I felt frozen. My brain had stopped working for a moment, like one of those times you are in the car and can't remember where you are or to what place you are going.

"I understand that the law recognizes a person's life as being more valuable."

"I didn't ask you your understanding of the law, I asked you your personal opinion about this."

I looked at David. He was staring intently at me from the defense table, with his head resting on his tented fingers. We had discussed this and discussed this and I had agreed that my response to anyone asking this question should be to agree with the premise that a person's life is always more valuable than a dog's. But, when I opened my mouth to speak, nothing came out.

Morales moved closer and spoke louder.

"Mr. Quintana … please answer my question," she pressed.

I sighed.

"Dogs are not … people, Ms. Morales … I know that. I respect that. But, I think everything has a right to live and not to suffer."

"Listen to my question, please. Do you or do you not think that a dog's life, YOUR dog's life in particular, was as important as that of Wendell Pruitt?!"

Morales voice rose with dramatic flair as she raised her arm toward the jury, her palm upward like supplication to the heavens. She must have practiced this gesture for weeks.

Finally I spoke. "I don't know."

Morales looked at me with practiced wide-eyed wonder.

"YOU DON'T KNOW?!!! You don't know if the life of a DOG is more important than that of a HUMAN BEING!"

She turned and looked at the jury with an expression of dismay.

I leaned forward and tried to speak calmly.

"What if the person is going to hurt a dog, your dog, for no reason, except to torture it and cause it to suffer? Doesn't the law say you have the right to protect members of your family?"

Morales attacked, like a hungry jaguar.

"So, you consider your DOG to be the same as a human member of your family."

"No, I didn't ... I don't ... know ... "

My face was getting hot and my heart was starting to beat like a drum. And then, I felt it, a force like a fist in my head, slowly unclenching and revealing an amazing truth. I sat up straight and looked Morales in the eye.

"YES, Lupe is a member of my family. I love her like a member of my family. And I will protect her as if she were a human member of my family! Morales was stunned into silence. Even she hadn't expected me to say this. The courtroom was abuzz with whispering. I knew everything had been lost, and I could not bear to look at David or Maria. I looked directly at Morales.

"So, Mr. Quintana, let me get this straight. You believe that it is okay for a person like you, who loves his dog and considers it a member of his family, to defend that animal's life at any cost, including killing another human being?"

"I can only say what I believe about myself and Lupe."

"So, then, do you think that it was justifiable homicide, the death of Wendell Pruitt?"

The courtroom was hushed. I took a deep breath. I looked from my hands slowly to Monica Morales' eyes, glaring at me like two brown laser beams.

"Yes."

The courtroom erupted into gasps and I heard Pruitt's sister scream out, "You Bastard!" I looked up and could see some people in the gallery arguing with each other and the local priest staring at me dourly and shaking his head.

The judge gaveled the courtroom into order, and it took about 30 seconds before silence was restored.

"Do you have any further questions, Ms. Morales?" the judge asked tiredly.

Morales dramatically slammed shut her notebook with a sharp "CLAP" and straightened her spine.

"No, your honor. I'm done!"

She walked back to her table and I could see that that she "high-fived" her assistant under the table. Apparently, the judge witnessed this too, and she frowned. She called Morales to the stand and hissed, "Ms. Morales … don't ever do that again … "

I finally glanced over to David, who looked very pale and small at the big oak defense table. He was a bit slumped in his chair, staring at his notes. Maria was sitting on the edge of her seat, her head tilted down at the floor. I know I had made a huge tactical error, I had ignored advice of counsel, and I had undermined my whole case. But, strangely enough, the rush of guilt and remorse I usually felt when I made a rash or poorly designed decision did not overwhelm me. I actually felt quite calm and serene. I had told the truth. I had been honest about who I was and what I knew to be right. I had saved a life. And, yes, Lupe's life was one that mattered to me. And she was a dog.

"Mr. Rubin, any redirect?"

David rose and approached me.

"Yes, your honor."

"Mr. Quintana, let me go over one more time with you your understanding of what happened at the time you pulled the trigger of your gun. You had testified that you did not remember the exact moment you did this?"

"No, I didn't. I don't."

"You remember getting a gun to scare Mr. Pruitt into letting your dog go, correct?"

"Yes."

"And you remember Mr. Pruitt putting the tip of a knife against Lupe's throat?"

"Yes."

"You remember him pushing the knife into her throat and blood coming out?"

"Yes."

"And the next thing you remember is seeing Mr. Pruitt bleeding and Lupe lying on the ground?"

"Yes."

"So, you don't remember actually engaging in any action that resulted in the death of Mr. Wendell Pruitt?"

"No. I don't."

"So, whether or not you believe that your actions may have been justified in your mind, you still maintain that you do not remember pulling the trigger?"

"Yes. I do."

"Thank you, your honor. Nothing further."

"Any re-cross Ms. Morales?"

Morales rose, with a smile still affixed to her lips.

"No re-cross, your honor."

She was probably rehearsing her closing argument already, painting me as a left-wing, animal rights radical who not only does not respect the rule of law, but had no understanding of the ethical difference between people and animals. I would be labeled immoral, ungodly, a danger to a civilized society.

I returned to my seat next to David, and the judge asked "Any further witnesses Mr. Rubin?"

"No, your honor."

"Then, we will reconvene at 10 a.m. tomorrow for closing arguments. I will give each of you an hour, and then I will give instructions to the jury and hopefully they will begin deliberations by late tomorrow."

Judge Tsosie looked at me with what appeared to be a kind expression. Of course, the judge might be pitying me, an old man, unable to keep his mouth shut, soon to be spending his remaining days in prison.

The courtroom emptied and Maria, David and I walked silently out the back door and to the parking lot. I readied myself for their disappointment and disapproval. Finally, David spoke.

"Anastasio, I know that was very hard on you. I understand also why you said what you said."

He stopped and I turned to look at him.

"I honestly respect what you did. I know I am a lawyer who is expected to win each and every case. We slant the truth here and there and muddy the waters to confuse the jury. My job is to get you an acquittal. And I won't lie and tell you that today will make that any easier."

Suddenly, David had tears in his eyes. He grabbed my arm.

"But, Tacho, you are a GOOD MAN. I admire you a great deal. Your honesty and love for Lupe just astonishes me. And humbles me … "

Then he looked at Maria who was standing by his side.

"For most of my life, I didn't have a father to look up to. But, honest to God, I would have been honored to have you as my father."

Maria started crying and when I reached for her she quickly moved away. I know that people in the parking lot had stopped to stare at this unseemly spectacle. We finally pulled ourselves together.

David composed himself and then good-naturedly pointed his finger at me.

"I will see you tomorrow. And, keep your hopes up!"

Maria and I walked silently to the truck. As we settled into the seats and I started the engine, Maria finally turned to me.

"Papi. I can't say that I think you were a wonderful father. You know you weren't. But I understand you so much more now. I know what it was like for you with Mami, and I know that you have had a lot of pain and disappointment in your life. But, with Lupe, I can finally see how much love survived in you. I … I … never expected that."

I touched her face with my hand.

"If you think that I love only Lupe with all my heart, you are wrong."

Maria stared at me for a moment; confused, happy, frozen … and then I could see a dark cloud pass in front of her eyes. She turned to look out the window.

We drove home silently. I didn't know what she was thinking, but perhaps it was the pain of realizing how many years we had wasted being alone together.

Lupe greeted us with the usual joy and unbridled enthusiasm that was her calling card. Hysterical jumping, barking and licking. A canine "Hallelujah." We went inside and closed the door. It felt good to be home.

Chapter 21

I slept fitfully that night. I wondered how it was that God would allow me to finally find myself, know my daughter for the first time, have Lupe safe and sound, and face a life sentence in prison. What was the reasoning behind this? What lesson should I be learning? Was I being punished? But, then, I have never really been a religious or God-fearing man. Long ago, since I was a child really, I realized that terrible things happen to people, sometimes wonderful things too, but none of it is destined. These things just happen. Luck. Chance. Fate. Whatever.

But, as I lay there, in the dark and silence with Lupe by my side, I began to realize that I wasn't angered by this strange twist of fate, but actually thankful … thankful that I had not died before I was able to appreciate life. All the awful things I had endured as a child and all the pain I had inflicted on myself these many years, had somehow not destroyed me. My spirit had been asleep, patiently waiting for something to awaken it.

I suddenly thought of the nature special I had watched some months before. The one about the Manzanita tree seeds that must be scorched by a fire before they can start to grow. I turned the information over and over in my head for some time, finally smiling when I realized that … it was me. I was the Manzanita seed!

When I awoke the next morning, I felt amazingly at peace. I couldn't change what would happen now. I feared it, of course, but not in the way I used to fear everything and everyone. I could feel the newly awakened

Manzanita, stirring and pushing, trying to break through the scarred shell that had been Anastasio Quintana.

I got up early and watched the sun rise over the Sandia with Lupe by my side. She was, as always, calm and at peace when I was with her. I felt her next to me like a boulder … unmovable, unshakable and … ever-present. I patted her head and we sighed in unison.

Maria and I didn't talk much at breakfast. She straightened out my tie, as usual, busied herself in the kitchen, and then we were off to Court. We met David in the courthouse parking lot and we all walked together to the courtroom, with heavy hearts.

At 10 o'clock, Judge Tsosie was announced, the jury filed in and the trial began its final stage. The judge looked tired, and she nodded at the prosecutor and then me with a blank expression.

"Ms. Morales, are you ready to present your closing argument?"

David had explained that the prosecutor always gets the first shot at arguing her case after the close of evidence. Morales was dressed from head to toe in a bright, obviously expensive, turquoise outfit. It had matching turquoise earrings and necklace, as well as turquoise-toned shoes—quite a bit brighter and bolder than anything she had yet worn to trial. She probably assumed that the verdict would be instantaneous and this would be her big day in front of the cameras, triumphantly representing justice and the rule of law.

As she got up, Morales glanced at me for a moment and, strangely, I suddenly found myself smiling at her. I don't know why, but I didn't feel the contempt for her that had so far consumed me during the trial. Morales was just doing what she had to do. Morales appeared puzzled by my grin and looked away from me quickly.

Walking to the podium, Morales put down her notes and took a moment to compose herself. She cleared her throat and began with a bit of a tremble in her voice.

"May it please the court, ladies and gentlemen of the jury, we have just spent the better part of a week listening to testimony from many witnesses, experts, neighbors, police, family and the defendant, Anastasio Quintana. What we now know is clear. We know that, on the day of April 10 of this year, Mr. Quintana, in his alleged effort to protect his DOG … (Morales said DOG with emphasized sarcasm and waited a moment to let it sink in) … shot and killed one Wendell Pruitt with a bullet to the brain. Mr. Pruitt, we know, did not have a gun and may have only held a knife. We know that he was across a five-foot high fence from Mr. Quintana at the time his death and would have been unable to harm Mr. Quintana in any way. We know from Mr. Quintana's own admissions that he did not fear for his own life, but that he feared only for the life of his DOG. We know that, and the defendant admits this … that he shot Wendell Pruitt to protect this DOG from harm."

Morales leaned forward and scanned the jurors' faces.

"What we have heard from witnesses is that Mr. Quintana had a temper, he had once engaged in a physical altercation at work, he had been a chronic alcoholic, and he had a history of hating Wendell Pruitt. Mr. Quintana owned a gun and kept it loaded for the purpose of protecting himself against burglars. At least that is what he said it was for. And, on the day of Wendell Pruitt's death, Mr. Quintana went into his own house, took his **loaded** gun, walked out of his house, took aim at Wendell Pruitt and killed him. With a single well-aimed gunshot to the brain."

Morales let this gruesome image sink in for a moment.

"Perhaps Mr. Quintana had just had enough of this annoying neighbor's bothersome behavior. He was angry. The man had taken his property, had been allegedly cruel to his wife, had been noisy and disruptive. The taking of his dog was the final straw and he decided it was time to act. He needed to finally stop the man who was making his life difficult. This is a reasonable conclusion given the facts. And killing a person because he is annoying is called murder."

Morales moved closer to the jury.

"However, EVEN IF Mr. Quintana did in fact shoot Mr. Pruitt to protect his DOG, and not solely for revenge, the law in New Mexico does not permit a person to take a human life to protect or defend the life of an animal. Simply put, even if Mr. Quintana found that his DOG's life had been put in jeopardy by Mr. Pruitt, even if Mr. Quintana acted only to save the life of his DOG, the law does not permit him to kill a person, a person who was posing no risk of harm to him. However you view the evidence, Mr. Quintana's actions clearly constitute criminal action, whatever his motive."

"Now, Mr. Quintana's defense is that he was not competent at the time of the actual firing of the gun."

Morales hesitated, shook back her hair and started to slowly walk back and forth in front of the jury box.

"Our expert witness, Dr. Ogilvy, explained that Mr. Quintana understood perfectly well what he did when he shot Mr. Pruitt. Was he upset, was he angry? Probably yes. But did he suffer a bout of "temporary amnesia" at the exact moment he pulled the trigger. You get to decide. But keep in mind that Mr. Quintana remembered getting the gun and aiming it at Mr. Pruitt. When he confronted the police officers later, he told them that he had killed Mr. Pruitt and that the gun was in the backyard. One would think that if Mr. Quintana did not remember shooting his gun, he would not have known who killed Mr. Pruitt, or what had happened to the gun."

"Did any of the evidence indicate that Mr. Quintana had suffered from temporary insanity or hysterical amnesia in the past? No. Suddenly he experiences, for the first time in his life, amnesia, and only at the very moment he actually kills someone. Kinda hard to swallow, isn't it?"

Morales tilted her head quizzically.

"Now, Mr. Quintana's expert witness, Dr. Ortiz, who was paid by the defendant to testify that the claimant did not know what he was doing at the time of the murder, claims in fact … that he didn't know what he was doing! No surprise. But, could you really say that she was any more credible than the prosecution's expert? Perhaps she went to better schools, maybe published more articles. I won't dispute that. But, Dr. Ortiz admitted that she only spoke to Mr. Quintana for a couple of hours. Two hours! Is this enough time to offer such an emphatic opinion? Actually, doesn't Dr. Ogilvy's testimony make ***more sense*** that that of Dr. Ortiz?"

"The only thing standing between Mr. Quintana and a guilty verdict is the ridiculous notion that, because of his emotional attachment to a DOG, he had a short period of temporary insanity, but only when he pulled the trigger of his gun. This defense does not constitute reasonable doubt, because it is so hard to believe it cannot be true."

"Whatever your feelings about Mr. Quintana, his life, his family or his DOG, or however you may feel about Mr. Pruitt's allegedly bad behavior, you must separate your feelings from the facts you have heard."

Morales stopped pacing and faced the jurors.

"Ladies and gentlemen of the jury. Do your job, follow the law. Find the defendant GUILTY."

With that final flourish, Morales breathed a huge sigh of relief and walked back to the prosecution table. She sat down, and glanced at the jury to see if she could read their reaction. I admit that I did too. I did not see any head nodding or shaking, any smiling or grimacing. They all appeared to be wearing their passive game-faces.

The judge turned slowly to David. "Mr. Rubin?"

"Thank you, your honor."

David buttoned his jacket, straightened his tie and rose to his full five feet nine inches. Before he strode toward the jury, he grabbed my shoulder and squeezed it hard. I looked at him and knew that he would do everything he could for me.

"Your Honor. Ladies and gentlemen of the jury. You have carefully and patiently listened to the evidence in this case and you have a difficult decision to make, one that will have lasting consequences for many people. This case is not as simple and straightforward as the prosecutor would have you believe. It is, in fact, quite complex, and perhaps the first of its kind. It is your duty **NOT** to make a rash and rushed decision, but to carefully examine and consider how all the various pieces of information fit together."

"Now, what we do know is that Wendell Pruitt was not a nice person. He was, in fact, a plague to his neighborhood … a bully and a lawbreaker. He was inconsiderate, threatening and destructive. A criminal. An aggressor. While the police tried to respond to the neighbors' serious complaints about Pruitt's behavior, no one was ever able to stop his cruelty and nuisance."

"Now, my client admittedly did not like Wendell Pruitt, and you would be hard-pressed to find anyone in San Sebastian that did not feel the same way. But Anastasio Quintana minded his own business and did his best not to provoke this beast of a man, even after Wendell Pruitt cursed at and insulted his wife, Raquel, and cruelly cheered her death. Certainly, if Mr. Quintana was as violent and dangerous a man as alleged by the prosecutor, he would have taken the law into his own hands well before April 10."

David glanced at Morales and then back to the jury.

"I think all of you will agree that the prosecutor's efforts to malign the character of Mr. Quintana fell flat. The best character witness the prosecution could find to testify was Cora Espinoza, sister-in-law of Mr. Quintana. This 'star' prosecution witness, who had known my client for decades, was unable to substantiate any violent or dangerous tendencies in Mr. Quintana. Her statements, quite frankly, were shown to be patently untrue and manufactured out of spite. Mr. Quintana's co-worker, Isidro

Baca and his daughter, Maria Quintana, testified much more forcefully and credibly that he was a troubled, yet peaceful and non-violent man."

David now walked so that he was standing beside me.

"So, here we have a good man, Anastasio Quintana … hardworking, humble, responsible, quiet … and a bad man, Wendell Pruitt, cruel, callous, violent and, dare I say, evil."

"Now, what really happened on April 10 between these two men? What we know is that Mr. Quintana had rescued an abused dog with whom he had a very loving relationship. Whether you consider this normal is not the point. My client, who suffered from a loveless abusive childhood and a thoroughly unhappy adult life, found redemption … in a dog. This dog gave him love, forgave him for his shortcomings, depended on him for affection and changed the course of his life. This dog, Lupe, was a miracle. She allowed Anastasio Quintana to love again, to find himself worthy of respect and to have a reason to exist. No small thing for a person of any age, but amazing for a man of 62."

"On April 10, every beautiful thing that Anastasio Quintana had found through Lupe was threatened. When Wendell Pruitt grabbed the dog, threatened to kill her and then pushed his knife into her throat, this represented to my client the potential loss of everything that mattered to him. Anastasio Quintana knew that Wendell Pruitt was not a man who could be reasoned with. He knew that all his pleading would do no good. He knew that waiting for the police to arrive would have come too late to save Lupe. My client did the only thing he thought could help save his beloved dog. He decided to threaten Wendell Pruitt with a gun that he had safely stored to protect his family. Yet, even this did not deter Wendell Pruitt from continuing his taunts, ridicule and threats, or from finally stabbing Lupe. What happened next was pivotal."

David moved closer to the jury and faced them head-on.

"First, let's address the issue of what we lawyers call 'mens rea.' This Latin phrase means, essentially, that a person has a knowing understanding of what he is doing. When we brush our teeth or put on our shoes, we are aware of our actions and can stop if we want to. In this case, you heard evidence from an eminent and well-respected board-certified psychiatrist, Dr. Melanie Ortiz, that Mr. Quintana suffered from a dissociative episode at the time directly before and after he shot Mr. Pruitt."

"As Dr. Ortiz explained it, there are occasions when people find themselves at such a high degree of panic and intense level of fear, that they lose the ability to understand where they are and what they are doing. She had not only read about this psychological state, but treated many patients who have suffered from it. So it is real, not theoretical. It is medically proven."

I could see that the jury was listening carefully, closely watching David as they tried to absorb what he was saying.

"In Mr. Quintana's case, this shy, troubled and mild-mannered man was suddenly forced to confront his worst fear, something that in his mind would utterly destroy him ... the brutal murder of his dog Lupe. The fears from his tragic childhood, the pain from his emotional isolation as an adult and the recent rebirth of hope all mixed together in a single horrifying moment."

David's voice took on a dramatic quality, like the radio personalities I had listened to as a child.

"Anastasio Quintana was face to face with Wendell Pruitt, who he fully believed was about to kill his dog in front of his eyes. My client pointed a gun at Mr. Pruitt to intimidate him, but not to kill him. But at that moment, when Lupe was stabbed, when her blood was flowing, when her life was about to end, his rational brain shut off and he did something primal, instinctual and without conscious thought. Mr. Quintana's mind and body separated from each other and it was as if another person had taken over him. Someone who had to protect him from destruction."

David waited a moment before going on.

"Dr. Ortiz explained this carefully and thoughtfully. After treating hundreds of patients, she described herself as an expert at dissimulation, or more simply put, lying, and found Mr. Quintana to be credible and truthful. Dr. Ortiz diagnosed him with a transitory dissociative disorder, which is included in medical literature, including the bible of psychiatry, the Dictionary and Statistical Manual of Psychiatric Disorders. Dr. Ortiz offered a meaningful explanation for Mr. Quintana's state of mind as well as his actions. According to Dr. Ortiz, there was no 'mens rea' at the time the trigger was pulled. No conscious understanding or awareness of his actions at that moment."

David smiled mockingly.

"As for Dr. Ogilvy, whose practice and livelihood are now exclusively limited to testifying for the prosecution in criminal trials, clearly did NOT perform a careful, thorough or even credible evaluation. It also appears that Dr. Ogilvy exaggerated his credentials, which are minimal, the amount of time he spent with Mr. Quintana, and his experience in dissociative impairments. Dr. Ogilvy, simply put, was not convincing or truthful and his testimony should be ignored as having no merit whatsoever."

"Your job, ladies and gentlemen of the jury, is to give greater weight to the medical opinion that you found more credible and that, undeniably, was the testimony of Dr. Melanie Ortiz. In fact her testimony, contrasted with that of Dr. Ogilvy, is like comparing Albert Einstein to a street-corner fortune teller."

"Lastly, I would ask you to not to give undue weight to the response of my client to one of the prosecutor's questions. Ms. Morales asked Mr. Quintana whether he was happy that his dog was alive, even though Mr. Pruitt was dead. He said yes. This may shock some of you, given that our society's traditional view of animals is that they are hardly more important than … an outdoor grill, a new suit or a wide-screen TV. But, Mr. Quintana did not see Lupe that way. To him, she was more than a piece of property."

David motioned to me with his arm, looking at me sympathetically.

"To Mr. Quintana, Lupe was a family member, a much loved companion and the joy of his life. She had given him a sense of belonging, greatly diminishing his despair, his self- hatred and his loneliness. To Mr. Quintana, the loss of Lupe would have been the equivalent of the loss of a family member, or of his own life. This was Mr. Quintana's truth on April 10, whether or not it is yours. On this matter, you must try to put your personal opinions aside."

"Was it awful what Mr. Pruitt did to Mr. Quintana's dog? Yes. Is it terrible that Mr. Pruitt lost his life. Of course. Is it terrible that Mr. Quintana did what he did? Absolutely. But, ask yourself, should we make this situation even more horrifying by sending Mr. Quintana to prison? Does he need to be punished? Does he need rehabilitation? Will he ever confront this situation again? The answer to all these questions is 'NO.' Please look into your hearts and minds and find him NOT GUILTY. Thank you."

With that, David walked to the table and sat down quietly beside me. I turned to see Maria, and she was smiling, her eyes moist. I leaned over and whispered into David's ear.

"Whatever happens, David, I have never been so grateful to anyone in my life. Gracias!"

The judge let us take a ten-minute break and I asked if David and Maria could just let me sit in the side room alone. I desperately wanted to hear nothing … just silence. No words about me, no recollections of Wendell Pruitt, no discussion about legal principles. I just wanted to be left alone until I could finally go home, go to bed and to sleep for two weeks. And if the decision was to send me to prison, I hoped I would at least get to say goodbye to Lupe.

Chapter 22

When we reconvened in Court, I noticed that Morales had an older grey-haired gentleman sitting beside her at the prosecution table. David identified him as the Sandoval County District Attorney himself, Ruben Gurule, probably called in by Morales to witness her great victory in court. Neither of them glanced over at me, as they and other staff from the DA's Office were busy laughing, poking each other in the shoulders and huddling together smiling.

On our side, the mood was quite different. Maria was sitting quietly behind me, in her usual front row seat, back straight, expressionless and a bit pale. I could see the familiar defiant faces of some animal rights people, the quietly pained and disapproving expression of the parish priest, as well as the usual motley assortment of Wendell Pruitt's friends and family members, looking angry and threatening.

David nervously doodled on his legal pad. He had already explained that the judge would now issue instructions to the jury and that he and Morales had already submitted proposed instructions, probably very different in form and substance.

Morales wanted the jury to consider both manslaughter AND second degree murder, while David wanted to eliminate second degree murder and the manslaughter charges and have the jury decide that I had only committed a lesser crime, like assault or improper discharge of a firearm. If the jury decided I had, in fact, lied about everything and shot Pruitt through the head knowing full well that I was going to kill the man, they could conceivably convict me of second-degree murder and I might spend the rest of my life in prison.

It was all very complicated and I tried my hardest to understand all the different ways other people could describe or characterize my actions. I had tried to explain, in my own words, what had happened, but I guess it was up to twelve strangers to decide who I was, what I had done and why.

The judge came into the courtroom, met at sidebar with the attorneys for some time and David returned to let me know that the judge had decided to allow the second degree murder charge in addition to the lesser charges. Morales looked confident.

So, I could be convicted of second-degree murder, voluntary manslaughter, assault with a deadly weapon or illegal discharge of a firearm. Or I could be acquitted as a result of temporary insanity. I felt strangely calm. There really was nothing more that David or I could do about my fate. We had done everything possible. It would be up to these other people and I would simply have to live with it.

The judge carefully gave the jury its instructions and dismissed the two alternate jurors, one of whom was an elderly Anglo lady who had stared at me rather sourly from time to time during the trial. At this, I felt a small measure of relief.

The jury was sent to deliberate and the judge left the room. The audience started talking, moving around and eventually leaving and David exited the court to make some phone calls. Maria and I were escorted into the side room and we chatted about little things … the hideous vomit-green dress that Wendell Pruitt's sister was wearing that day, the darkening clouds, signaling a rare rain, and about Lupe.

It was almost an hour when the judge came back in to let us know that the jury was going to go home and resume deliberating the next morning. Court was dismissed and we filed out, with heavy hearts and the desire to think about anything but tomorrow. Maria and David talked privately for a while before he left.

Everyone appeared to be talking to the press, and I saw one reporter interviewing a woman wrapped in what looked like a garbage bag, holding a sign that said "Animals are People too." Even the other animal rights people didn't want to be near her.

As Maria and I had almost reached the truck, we saw Wendell Pruitt's family walk out of the courthouse. When they saw me across the parking lot, one gave me "the finger" and Pruitt's sister pointed at me and then drew a slit across her throat. Then they all laughed raucously. Maria glared at them, but neither of us said anything.

"He got what he deserved," I thought.

Chapter 23

The jury deliberated for four days. Twice we rushed down to the courthouse to find that they just wanted to ask the judge for clarifications on the law. David told me that it was nothing to worry about.

As I understood it, if the jurors could not reach a consensus for a verdict of guilty or not guilty, we would probably have to have another entire trial. This seemed even crueler than a guilty verdict.

During those long four days, Maria, Lupe and I settled into the house and only went out to shop for food. A moderately-sized crowd had gathered, including some nitwits who had apparently listened to one of the local radio show lunatics spend a whole morning decrying me as a savage murderer, a tool of radical extremists and a crusader for the rights of dogs and people to marry. They carried signs that said "Animals are for Eating" and "Save the Humans." Maria and I watched television, sat in the backyard when the weather was nice, and I was even able to take Lupe for a few walks, sneaking out before the sun came up. David suggested we stay away from people and not say anything to anyone.

Maria kept herself busy with housework, typing on her laptop computer and watching television. I, meanwhile, tried not to obsess about whether this might be the last night that I slept in a real bed, had the bathroom to myself or would be able to sit on the couch with Lupe's head on my lap. I had to believe we could win, or that I would only have to go to jail for a short time. Otherwise, I think I would have wept nonstop.

Finally, Friday, we got a call from David that the jury had finally reached a verdict. He told me that the longer a jury is out, the more likely there will be an acquittal. But, I knew he was feeling pessimistic and seemed very sad. Maria kept her distance from David and said very little to either of us. I could tell from the grayish cast to her skin and the dark circles under her eyes that she had not been sleeping.

When we got to court, Morales was there, complete with assistants, District Attorney Gurule and half the prosecutor's office in back of her. She glanced at me quickly and nodded to David, but otherwise seemed preoccupied with how her hair looked, twisting it into a ponytail over and over. Perhaps she was nervous too.

The judge arrived, with the same neutral expression as always, and called the court to order. The jury filed in and I looked carefully at their faces. I had read in a book, or maybe I watched it on a TV episode of "Law and Order," that jurors who had decided to convict would not look at the defendant. I noted that they glanced at their laps and at the judge, but not at me. My fear started to rise.

At last the court was silent. The judge rose.

"Jury forewoman, has the jury reached a verdict?"

The jury forewoman, a young Latina who had taken copious notes throughout the trial, stood up. Yes, your honor. Her voice quavered. My heart pounded so hard that it felt as though it was going to crack my ribs. My throat was dry and my head hurt terribly. I closed my eyes and heard the judge ask the clerk to bring her the verdict.

When I opened my eyes again a moment later, the judge was carefully reading the verdict. She then folded it up and sent it back to the jury forewoman. The judge looked at me, still no expression, and asked me to stand. I stood up on shaky legs and David stood beside me, gripping my shoulder.

The forewoman began.

"On the count of illegal discharge of a firearm, the jury finds Anastasio Quintana, GUILTY."

I knew right away that this was not going to be good. If I was found competent to have fired a gun, I would probably be deemed competent to have killed Wendell Pruitt. But I hoped. I still hoped …

"On the count of second degree murder, we the jury, found the defendant Anastasio Quintana, NOT GUILTY."

David squeezed my shoulder until it started to hurt. I raised my fist to my mouth. Could it be … !?

"On the count of voluntary manslaughter in the first degree, we the jury, find the defendant Anasastio Quintana, GUILTY."

I felt strangely numb at that moment, my mind without any emotion at all. But when I opened my mouth to breathe, I involuntarily gasped for breath. I did not look at the jury, judge or Morales, though I imagined the prosecutor was turning cartwheels in the aisle. I felt sorry for myself, but I felt worse for David, Maria and especially Lupe. I had pledged to take care of Lupe for the rest of her life and I knew she depended on me. I couldn't bear to be without her.

The judge gaveled for order. Morales found her way back to her table, beaming like an Olympic champion.

Judge Tsosie was silent for several moments as she appeared to compose herself. The courtroom slowly became quiet. I was hoping the judge wouldn't sentence me right now and have me put immediately into custody. I just needed to say goodbye. To my home. My life. My freedom. To Lupe.

At last, the judge started to speak.

"Before I discharge the jury, I have an important decision to make. I, too, have listened to the evidence in this case, heard the testimony of witnesses and followed the arguments of counsel. The jury was instructed to determine the guilt or lack of guilt of Mr. Quintana based on the 'beyond a reasonable doubt' standard, which as we all know, is a heavy burden on the prosecution. It is, indeed, up to the jury to apply the facts to the law and to render an impartial judgment based on their studied deliberation. It is their job in almost all criminal cases to render the final verdict based on their conclusions. The judge paused in the dead silence of the courtroom.

"However … "

Suddenly, I heard Morales loudly say, "NO!" and saw her freckled assistant pulling at her shoulder and whispering into her ear to try to calm her down.

The judge stared at Ms. Morales but said nothing. Finally, she went on.

"As I was saying, there are circumstances, rare as they are, when the evidence is so far from satisfying the standard of beyond a reasonable doubt, that the judge has an obligation to examine that decision and see if it comports with the very basic demands of justice. In this case, I do not believe that any credible evidence was entered contradicting or impeaching the testimony of Dr. Ortiz or supporting the prosecution's theory of the crime."

David looked like he was hurling down a rollercoaster. He face went pale, his mouth hung open and he was unblinking.

"In this case, the prosecution clearly failed to prove its case as demanded by our rigorous standard of proof. As a result, I have no choice but to overturn the jury's verdict and enter a verdict of 'not guilty' on all counts."

There was a brief moment of absolute silence, and then the courtroom was in an uproar. The DA was red-faced, talking loudly on his cell phone, Morales was surrounded by angry assistants and she seemed near tears. I looked to David quizzically …

"I don't understand … "

He turned to me.

"The judge did one of the most extraordinary things a judge can do, she 'tossed' the guilty verdict. Judges only do this very VERY rarely. I mean, I have never seen it happen in all my years as a criminal lawyer. Most judges never do it no matter what. But a brave judge can do this if she believes there was a basic miscarriage of justice. And this judge has balls!"

My heart suddenly sank.

"So, I will have to go through all this again with another judge and jury?"

"No, Anastasio!! That's it. No! Double jeopardy has applied. You can never be tried again for this crime. And the DA cannot, by law, appeal it. You are free!!"

He hugged me with great intensity and I could feel his heart racing. Maria ran through the swinging gates like a bull into a fight ring and threw her arms around me, crying.

The judge allowed the commotion to go on for a minute or so, but then gaveled everyone to their seats.

The DA himself rose. He pointed at Judge Tsosie.

"This is outrageous. You cannot do this, it is unconscionable. It's a sham. You have no right!!!"

The judge stood up behind the bench to her full 5'3" height. She looked impassive.

"Mr. Gurule. I CAN do this, I am empowered to do this and I feel I must do this. Check your law books and you'll find that every criminal court judge has such authority."

Pruitt's sister rose to her feet, shaking her fist.

"YOU DAMN INDIAN!"

Soon, others of the Pruitt crowd were shouting, "Go Back To the Reservation, Stupid Squaw," "This is Injun Revenge" and the like. It was ugly.

The animal rights people started screaming back at the Pruitt people and the San Felipe Indian juror stood up and pointed at Pruitt's sister, swearing.

The judge gaveled a few times for order, but the chaos was now beyond control. She turned to me, and said in a very calm voice, barely heard over the noise, "You are free to go, Mr. Quintana. Good luck to you."

Judge Bernice Tsosie then quietly disappeared from the courtroom through the door behind the bench.

David was still shaking his head. Maria was growing alarmed by the shouting and shoving in the courtroom. The court officers had their hands full, and she asked David if we could quickly go into the side room. He ushered us in, closed the door and had a court officer stand outside.

Once in the room, Maria looked at me, hugged me again and said, surprisingly,

"Lupe is going to be SOOOOOO happy!!!" I looked at her for a moment and then did something I hadn't done in a very long time ... I laughed.

A million thoughts were running through my head at once, but suddenly, they all fell away and only one remained. I turned to Maria. "Let's go home!"

Chapter 24

The furor didn't die down for over a week. Camera crews and reporters, apparently from all over the globe, were camped out at our house, peeking over the backyard fence, pointing their telescopic lenses into our windows. We left only at the dead of night, going to a 24-hour grocery store in Albuquerque for food. Sally Chavez and a few neighbors like Hortensia Vigil brought over food. I unplugged our phone and Maria bought a tracphone with an untraceable number.

Maria was drawn to the exploding news coverage of the trial, where quite a battle was raging between MSNBC and Fox over my acquittal. PETA had issued a statement calling me an American hero, and the national Republican Party chairman labeled me an outlaw and called the judge an affirmative action failure. The Sandoval County DA had filed a complaint against Judge Tsosie with the Judicial Review Board and it was reported that the judge had taken a leave of absence and gone to visit relatives on the reservation near Shiprock.

Morales, I heard, left on an extended vacation to Bali. I did not know what her future would be with the DA's office, but David said perception is everything in politics and her chances of winning political office, or rising to the top of the DA's staff, had been severely damaged.

The continuing raucous debate on radio and television centered on how an animal's life should be valued when measured against that of a human being. Some scientists argued that the "sentience" of animals suggested a need to explore innovative avenues of protection. New age gurus decried treatment of animals like property, and Bible thumpers ranted that animals had no soul and were nothing more than food and labor provided by God for people to use at will.

The Bishop of the local Catholic diocese called me an unrepentant sinner who would not go to heaven, while a congregation of nuns in Wisconsin proclaimed that I had done God's work and sent a big jar of homemade jam. Psychiatrists and psychologists discussed the temporary insanity defense; some dismissing it as bogus psychobabble and others citing the many empirical studies supporting it.

I received letters inviting me to appear on talk shows, including "Oprah" and "Larry King Live", and got daily delivery of scores of letters and notes, some wishing me well and others praying I would be shot myself. I was especially surprised when I received a note of congratulations from a well-known motorcycle gang from California.

"People Magazine" even wanted to put Lupe and me on the cover together.

Ordinarily, I would have been stunned, terrified and incredulous to find the whole world talking about me and debating my life. But the events of the past few months had changed me. I had seen the downside of sudden "fame" and now all I wanted was for everyone to go away. I longed to return to that brief period after I rescued Lupe when I had found peace. But, deep inside, I knew it would never be like that again.

And for the center of the controversy, Lupe, the only difference she saw in her life was disappointment that she couldn't go out on long walks every day. She spent many hours noisily barking at people knocking on the front door or crossing the lawn.

David did a few interviews on television, with my permission of course, but stopped after someone threw a hard plastic dog bone at his head. He called Maria daily, and I spoke with him a couple of times letting him know that I was fine. David reported to Maria that he had received several offers to appear regularly as a legal consultant on CNN, and had been approached by several high profile criminal defendants seeking representation. He told Maria that he was taking time to think about all that.

As for Maria, she went about her business, cleaning up, ironing, cooking, trying to stay busy. We talked, watched television together, gave Lupe a much-needed bath, and tried not to think too much about the future. I believed Maria was planning to return to Seattle, as I heard her whispering the city's name on her cell phone quite a bit. David, I knew, had fallen in love with her, and desperately wanted her to stay. Yet, Maria always held back her thoughts, pushed David away, never discussing the future with either of us.

Finally, after a couple of weeks, the press' attention span was exhausted and it moved on to yet another hot topic; the disappearance of a second-rate movie star at a cruise ship port of call. We were able to return to a semblance of our old life. I noticed the neighbors still avoided me and Maria, but many strangers drove to San Sebastian in the hope of including me and Lupe in their travel photos. Of course, the people who had been good to me throughout the whole ordeal, Benny and his wife Sally, Isidro, Hortensia, a few of my former co-workers, and some of the business people who had come to know my family over the years, offered their good wishes and support.

Lupe became a kind of mixed breed celebrity. Her photo appeared more often in the newspapers and tabloids that mine did! "The National Enquirer" even wrote an article that the FBI had been forced to hire a personal bodyguard for her (though I never saw any people with black suits, sunglasses and earpieces near the house). The "Albuquerque Journal" even ran a front-page photo of Lupe sleeping in the backyard next to her piece of blue rope.

Lupe didn't seem to care about her sudden fame; she just wanted to be with me. More than anything, Lupe's unfailing enthusiasm, devotion and optimism helped me to move on. I hoped that we might still be able to have a good life together.

However, I would once again be reminded how fickle life can be.

Chapter 25

Another week went by and Maria started to become anxious and fidgety. After doing some dusting and shopping each morning, she was at a loss as to how to fill the rest of her day. Lupe, Maria and I took long walks in nearby Placitas, and we tried to go out to dinner in Albuquerque once a week. A few people continued to stop by and check on us, and Maria and Sally had become good friends. Mostly, however, I think we made the locals uncomfortable.

David kept in daily contact with Maria and, though I knew she cared for him, there was something causing her to run from any deep involvement. David was obviously smitten with Maria, enough to keep on trying to win her over, but she would not commit to anything but a "dating" situation. I kept hearing her insist to him that they were "just great friends." Perhaps Maria really wanted to leave San Sebastian and was trying to spare David any pain, but I thought it more likely that she was continuing her legacy of pushing people away who got too close. A younger version of me.

Lupe had become the light of both of our lives. I would often come out of my room and find Maria on the couch watching television with Lupe's head in her lap. Maria insisted on getting the best canned dog food for Lupe, no dry food allowed, and spoiled her frequently with dog treats until we started to see Lupe's ribs disappear from view altogether. Lupe had the gift, as perhaps all dogs do, of allowing trusted people to feel as if they were the center of the universe.

A few days later, after Lupe and I returned from our walk, I found Maria sitting in the kitchen, staring into space. I could tell from the serious look on her face that she had something important to tell me. After petting Lupe and making me a cup of coffee, she told me that she had decided to go back to Seattle.

I nodded, an awful dagger of pain going through my chest. The old awkward moment. Do I hug her and plead for her to stay? Do I smile and say, "It's for the best"? Or do I simply thank her for helping me so much over the past few months? As usual, I just sat there, contemplating my options. Finally, I said, "Is that what you want?"

"Well yes, Papi. There really is nothing here for me … I mean there is you and Lupe of course, but I don't have a job, my friends are back in Washington, I don't feel like I belong here anymore."

"And David?"

Maria swirled around to face me, a look of shock on her face, as if I had just read the innermost secrets in her diary. I looked into her eyes silently. She turned away again nervously.

"David is wonderful, Papi. A terrific man. I … I am … he has his life and I have mine. I can't drop everything in the hope that …

Her voice trailed off and she stopped speaking.

"Maria, I understand."

I knew her well enough to know she meant "I can't risk falling in love with him. He'll really get to know me, the real me, angry and insecure, and that will be the end of that." Or maybe I had set the bar so low as a father that Maria did not believe any man could actually bring her any long-term happiness.

There was a long silence. Perhaps Maria had hoped I would make an enthusiastic pitch for her to remain with us, but we were still too uncomfortable with each other; still unwilling to risk rejection.

"Lupe will miss you," I said softly.

I saw Maria's eyes tear up.

"And I will miss that sweet little thing. Lupita, my love! Maria bent over to pat Lupe's head. Lulu, do you want a treat?"

I swallowed and took a deep breath.

"I'll miss you too, mija."

Maria looked at me somewhat startled, and then nodded.

"I know. I know." She started to say more, but again stopped.

"When are you leaving?"

"I think next week, I'll fly back and see if I can get back my old apartment. I heard it's still empty. I can stay with my friend Paula for awhile."

I felt deep sadness at the thought that Maria would be gone again. However, I must admit, I felt some relief too. No more dancing around our feelings for each other, avoiding anything and everything that might trigger anger, resentment or hope. But mostly, I felt concerned for her. I thought she might be turning into me, the old me … afraid of people—mistrustful and suspicious. And always finding excuses not to change and to be alone.

We spent the evening quietly watching television, taking turns rubbing Lupe's belly, as she had shamelessly lain down between us on the couch, on her back, her four legs spread open to the world. If only people could learn such trust.

Awhile later, just before bedtime, I let Lupe out in the backyard. Within about ten minutes, she soon started barking and I heard motorcycles revving their engines nearby. I went to the door and called Lupe, but she continued barking. I went out the back door to check on her and, by the dim glow of the streetlight, I saw a big tattooed man, with a full white beard and a bandana on his head, peering over the top of the fence.

I called Lupe more loudly and urgently, and Maria came behind me to see what was happening. At that moment, I saw the man reach over the fence with one arm. Suddenly, I heard the thunderous sound of gun firing, three times, with flashes like fireworks. The man quickly disappeared from the fence and I heard shouting and whooping as the motorcycles quickly tore off down the street.

I ran to the middle of the backyard and stopped. Lupe was no longer barking. Then, I spotted her about ten yards from the fence, lying on the ground. My legs suddenly felt like they were 20 years old again and I ran like an Olympic sprinter towards her. I later learned that I was screaming Lupe's name at the top of my lungs, heard by neighbors all the way over on Valverde Street. By the time I got to where Lupe was and threw myself next to her on the ground, I knew that she was dead. There was blood all over her fur, her chest was not moving and her head was turned oddly to one side. I grabbed her limp body and pulled her toward me, cradling her head next to mine. Screaming her name. Over and over. I felt as though

I was dying. I felt horrifying pain, agony, helplessness. I wanted to die. I wanted not to exist.

Suddenly Maria was at my side, sobbing, holding Lupe, and I saw that she was now covered with blood. My daughter cried like I had never seen her cry before. She wailed like a baby, desperate, afraid, begging for help. I looked at her at that moment, so vulnerable and so small and I reached behind her and hugged her. Maria looked up at me, her face smeared with blood, and threw her arms around me. She cried, "Papi, Papi ... !!!!," over and over, tears streaming down her face.

I hugged her closer and cried, "I am so sorry, mija. I am so sorry I was such a bad father. So sorry that I wasn't around when you needed me. I wish I could go back and change it. I wish I could be your father again."

Maria kept crying and hugged me even tighter.

"But I'm here now, Maria. I am here for you. I love you. I LOVE YOU." I found that I was shouting.

Maria buried her head in my shoulder for a minute and then looked up at me, her eyes wet and shining, her hair tangled and clothes stained and matted with Lupe's blood.

She gulped, trying to catch her breath.

"I LOVE YOU TOO, PAPI!

We sat there holding each other for what seemed like hours. Neither of us wanted to let go. It was as if we needed to catch up on all the years we had missed each other. Finally, my heart breaking into pieces, I pick up Lupe's limp body and we carried her inside. Later that night, the rain came and washed away the blood on the ground.

They never found the people who killed Lupe. I called the police and an officer came over to take a report, but I could tell that no one was going to do anything. After all, Lupe was just a dog and they weren't going to start going after motorcycle gang members to investigate the death of an animal. Nothing had changed.

Maria and I buried Lupe at dawn the next day, in a small meadow at the foot of the mountain in Placitas, Lupe's favorite place to hike. I put her favorite toys next to her, including the faded and frayed blue rope, and we marked her grave with a large stone we rolled over from a nearby hill. I will always remember where Lupe's grave is ... it is next to the old rangy cottonwood tree where we sometimes took summer naps together in the shade.

Reporters and television crews once again converged on us, camping out on the lawn for a few days, trying to get photos of me or Maria. Finally, David called a press conference and issued a statement condemning the cowardice that would make someone kill a defenseless animal. He insisted that the police catch the killers and the District Attorney's Office pursue felony charges against the assailants. The police did little, the DA said nothing. No one was ever caught.

The commotion quickly died down. We received hundreds of condolence letters and dozens of hate letters. But the most important letter I received was a very touching note from Judge Tsosie, who offered her sympathies and included a Navajo proverb, **"You cannot see the future with tears in your eyes."**

It is one of the few things I will always carry with me.

Despite our sadness and grief over the loss of our beloved Lupe, Maria and I had turned a corner. We were able to talk to each other without the caution and distance that had always characterized our relationship. We discussed painful memories of the past, our disappointments and anger, and reached a place where I think we could begin to build new, good memories as father and daughter.

Most importantly, I think that Lupe's death finally released Maria from her fear of loss, her terror of being abandoned and forgotten, and the inability to express her pain. She knew she could and would survive.

We talked about David. She told me that she loved him and had been afraid to be with him for fear that he would abandon her or that he would be disappointed in her. I advised her not to make my mistake. Not to let fear and anger rule her life. Not to be afraid to change.

After all, Lupe had come suddenly and unexpectedly into my life, bringing me nothing but joy, releasing me from my prison of self-loathing and loneliness. Without Lupe, I would have been the same dead soul that I had been for so much of my life.

It was only a few days after Lupe's murder that Maria announced she was going to stay in Albuquerque to live with David and was going to start looking for a job. She was the happiest I have seen her in many years. The next time I saw David, he looked at me with such a big smile, I half expected him to do a back flip and then leap into my arms. I told David that I would be proud and honored to have him as my son-in law.

You might think this odd, even crazy, but I had meanwhile decided to leave San Sebastian and start a new life far away from all the memories and pain. I gave Maria the responsibility of selling my house and everything in it, and, while she was deeply disappointed I had decided to leave, she said she understood. Even though we would be apart physically, she knew now that I would never abandon her again.

I had decided to head to California after watching a travel show on television about the endless miles of beaches, tall redwood trees and deep blue lakes. I had always wanted to see an ocean sunset and to try sourdough bread (was it really sour?). I packed a couple of small boxes of clothes, pictures and household items and said my goodbyes to the few good friends I had made over the years. I also drove over to Lupe's grave, spent some time with her, and then buried a small statue of Our Lady of Guadalupe in a hole next to our tree. I didn't want Lupe to be lonely.

I also decided, perhaps impulsively, to stop by the Rio Rancho animal shelter. I had seen a scruffy, frightened dog, about five years old, featured in the "Albuquerque Journal" the day before. It had been picked up as a stray and had already spent months in a cage, waiting fruitlessly to be adopted. The photo showed a stout dog, short legs, with a collie- like snout, patchy fur and drooping ears, cowering against a counter and staring fearfully at the camera. When I came to look at the homely and scared dog in her barren cage, I loved her at first sight. Despite her shyness and fear, I could see that she still had a spark of hope in her eyes. I bent down, offered my hand, and to the shelter staff's surprise, she slowly came to me. When we left the shelter together, she jumped up into my truck and licked my hand. I decided at once to call her Manzanita. "Nita" for short.

When we get on the highway tomorrow and head west towards California, I know that I will never be lonely again.

Discussion Guide

1. What was unique about the setting of the book and how did it enhance or take away from the story?

2. What specific themes did the author emphasize throughout the novel? what do you think he was trying to get across to the reader?

3. Do the characters seem real and believable? can you relate to their predicaments? to what extent to they remind you of yourself or someone you know?

4. How do the characters change or evolve throughout the course of the story? what events trigger such changes?

5. In what ways do the events in the book reveal evidence of the author's world view?

6. Did certain parts of the book make you uncomfortable? is so, why did you feel that way? did this lead to a new understand or awareness of some aspect of your life or beliefs you might not have thought of before?

About the Author

Edward Goodman lives in Corrales, New Mexico with his partner Ennio and six canines, including his incredible dog Lupe. Ed has worked on and off as a newspaper features reporter and has practiced law for the last 26 years as a disability attorney. Born and raised in Binghamton, New York, Ed grew up with dogs, cats, gunea pigs, snakes, lizards, mice, and rabbits and developed a deep love and respect for animals. Ed graduated from the University of Rochester with bachelor's degrees in history and psychology and from law school at the University of Michigan. Ed lived for twenty years in Boston, MA before relocating to New Mexico in 2004. Ed was a finalist in the New Mexico Governors' screen writing competition with his story "Channeling Frida." This is Ed's first novel.